THE
BEACON SECOND
READER
BY
JAMES H. FASSETT

PREFACE

In the "Beacon Second Reader" the author has chosen for his stories only those of recognized literary merit; and while it has been necessary to rearrange and sometimes rewrite them for the purpose of simplification, yet he has endeavored to retain the spirit which has served to endear these ancient tales to the children of all ages. The fairy story appeals particularly to children who are in the second school year. It has been proved by our ablest psychologists that at about this period of development, children are especially susceptible to the stimulus of the old folklore. They are in fact passing through the stage which corresponds to the dawn of the human race, when demons, dragons, fairies, and hobgoblins were as firmly believed in as rivers and mountains.

As a test of this theory the author asked hundreds of second-grade and third-grade school children to recall the stories which they had read during the preceding year, and to express their preferences. The choice of more than ninety per cent proved to be either folklore stories, pure and simple, or such tales as contained the folklore element. To be sure, children like other stories, but they respond at once with sparkling eyes and animated voices when the fairy tale is suggested. How unwise, therefore, it is to neglect this powerful stimulus which lies ready at our hands! Even a pupil who is naturally slow will wade painfully and laboriously through a fairy story, while he would throw down in disgust an account of the sprouting of the bean or the mining of coal.

It can hardly be questioned, moreover, that the real culture which the child derives from these literary classics is far greater than that which he would gain from the "information" stories so common in the average second and third readers.

THE SHOEMAKER AND THE ELVES—I

sho emaker	b eautiful	to- morrow	l eather
alre ady	b ought	sew	e nough

A shoemaker and his wife lived in a little house on the edge of a wood.
They were very, very poor, and each day they grew poorer and poorer.
At last there was nothing left in the house but leather for one pair of shoes.
"I will cut out this last pair of shoes," the shoemaker said to his wife.
"To-morrow I will sew them and peg them."
So he cut out the leather and left it on his bench.
The next morning he went into his shop to make the shoes.
What did he see!
A pair of shoes, all nicely made and ready to be sold.
The stitches were so fine and the shoes so well made that they were quickly sold.
With the money the poor shoemaker bought leather for two pairs of shoes.
Then he said to his wife, "I will cut out the leather for two pairs of shoes.
To-morrow I will sew them and peg them."
So he cut out the leather for the shoes and left it on his bench.
The next morning when he went into his shop to make the shoes, what did he find!

Yes, there were two pairs of shoes already made.
The work was so well done that those shoes were also sold very quickly.
With the money the poor shoemaker bought enough leather for four pairs of shoes.
Those he also cut out and left it upon his bench.
The next morning he found four pairs of beautiful shoes, all well made.
And so it went on and on. Instead of being a very poor shoemaker, he became a very rich shoemaker.

His shoes were so well made that even the queen herself wore them.

THE SHOEMAKER AND THE ELVES—II

At last the shoemaker said to his wife, "We must find out who makes the shoes."

So one bright moonlight night they hid behind a curtain, where they could watch the bench and not be seen.

Just on the stroke of midnight, two little elves jumped through the window.

They went skipping and dancing up to the bench.

Sitting cross-legged they took up the leather and began to work.

How their needles flew back and forth, back and forth!

How their little hammers beat rap-a-tap-tap, rap-a-tap-tap!

Almost before the shoemaker and his wife could think, the work was all done.

The tiny elves ran about, skipping and dancing, skipping and dancing.

Then, whisk! quick as a wink, they were gone.

The next morning the good shoemaker said to his wife, "What can we do for those dear little elves?"

"I should like very much to make some clothes for them," said his wife. "They were almost naked."

"If you will make their coats, I will make them some shoes," said the shoemaker. "Their little feet were bare."

When the clothes and shoes were ready, they were put upon the bench.

The shoemaker and his wife again hid behind the curtain.

Just as before, when the clock struck twelve, in jumped the tiny elves.

They went skipping and dancing, skipping and dancing, to their work.

They saw the little coats, the tiny stockings, and the neat little shoes.

They clapped their hands for joy.

Then, slipping on their clothes, they skipped, hand in hand, out of the window.

The shoemaker and his wife never saw the little elves again, but after that night, good luck seemed always to be with them.

English Folk Tale

THE SHIP

aden	ove

I saw a ship a-sailing, A-sailing on the sea; And, oh, it was all laden With pretty things for thee!

There were comfits in the cabin, And apples in the hold; The sails were made of silk, And the masts were made of gold.

The four and twenty sailors That stood between the decks Were four and twenty white mice, With chains about their necks.

The captain was a duck, With a jacket on his back; And when the ship began to move, The captain said, "Quack! quack!"

Old English Rhyme

THE WOLF AND THE SEVEN YOUNG KIDS—I

q uietly	r ough	iece	s cissors
l earned	t hought	halk	y oungest

There was once an old goat who had seven little kids.

2

She loved them all as much as any mother ever loved her children.

One day the old goat wished to go into the woods to get food for her kids.

Before she started she called them all to her and said:

"Dear children, I am going into the woods.

Now do not open the door while I am away.

If the old wolf should get into our hut, he would eat you all up, and not a hair would be left.

You can easily tell him by his rough voice and his black feet."

"Dear mother," cried all the young kids, "we will be very careful not to let the old wolf in.

You need not think of us at all, for we shall be quite safe."

So the old goat went on her way into the dark woods.

She had not been gone long when there came a loud rap at the door, and a voice cried:

"Open the door, my dear children. I have something here for each of you."

But the young kids knew by the rough voice that this was the old wolf.

So one of them said, "We shall not open the door. Our mother's voice is soft and gentle. Your voice is rough. You are a wolf."

The old wolf ran away to a shop, where he ate a piece of white chalk to make his voice soft.

Then he went back to the goat's hut and rapped at the door.

He spoke in a soft voice and said, "Open the door for me, my dear children. I am your mother."

But the oldest little goat thought of what his mother had said.

"If you are our mother, put your foot on the window sill, that we may see it."

When the wolf had done this, all the little goats cried out, "No, you are not our mother. We shall not open the door. Our mother's feet, are white and yours are black. Go away; you are the wolf."

Then the wolf went to the miller's, and said to him, "Mr. Miller, put some flour on my foot, for I have hurt it."

The miller was so afraid of the wolf that he did as he was told.

Then the wicked wolf went to the goat's house again and said, "Open the door, dear children, for I am your mother."

"Show us your foot," said the little kids.

So the wolf put his one white foot on the window sill.

When the little kids saw that it was white, they thought this was really their mother, and they opened the door.

In jumped the ugly old wolf, and all the little kids ran to hide themselves.

The first hid under the table, the second in the bed, the third in the oven, the fourth in the kitchen, the fifth in the cupboard, the sixth under the washtub, and the seventh, who was the smallest of all, in the tall clock.

The wolf quickly found and gobbled up all but the youngest, who was in the clock.

Then the wolf, who felt sleepy, went out and lay down on the green grass.

Soon he was fast asleep.

THE WOLF AND THE SEVEN YOUNG KIDS—II

Not long after this the old goat came home from the woods.

Ah, what did she see! The house door was wide open; the tables and chairs were upset.

The washtub was broken in pieces, and the bed was tipped over.

"Where are my dear children?" cried the poor goat.

At last she heard a little voice crying, "Dear mother, here I am in the tall clock."

The old goat helped the little goat out.

Soon she learned how the wolf had eaten her dear children.

Then she went out of the hut, and there on the grass lay the wolf sound asleep.

3

As the goat looked at the wicked old wolf, she thought she saw something jumping about inside him.

"Ah," she said, "it may be that my poor children are still alive."

So she sent the little kid into the house for a pair of scissors and a needle and some thread.

She quickly cut a hole in the side of the wicked old wolf.

At the first snip of the scissors, one of the kids stuck out his head.

As the old goat cut, more and more heads popped out.

At last all six of the kids jumped out upon the grass.

They went hopping and skipping about their mother.

Then the old goat said to them, "Go and bring me some large stones from the brook."

The seven little kids ran off to the brook and soon came back with seven large stones. They put these stones inside the wicked old wolf.

The old goat sewed up the wolf's side so gently and quietly that he did not wake up nor move.

When at last the wicked wolf did wake up, the great stones inside him made him feel very heavy.

He was thirsty, too, so he walked down to the brook to drink.

The stones were so heavy that they tipped him over the edge of the bank into the deep water, and he was drowned.

WILLIAM AND JACOB GRIMM

THEY DIDN'T THINK

d		
anger	olks	eized

Once a trap was baitedWith a piece of cheese;It tickled so a little mouse,It almost made him sneeze.An old rat said, "There's danger,Be careful where you go!""Nonsense!" said the other,"I don't think you know!"So he walked in boldly—Nobody in sight—First he took a nibble,Then he took a bite;Close the trap togetherSnapped as quick as wink,Catching mousey fast there,'Cause he didn't think.

Once there was a robin,Lived outside the door,Who wanted to go insideAnd hop upon the floor."No, no," said the mother,"You must stay with me;Little birds are safestSitting in a tree.""I don't care," said Robin,And gave his tail a fling,"I don't think the old folksKnow quite everything."Down he flew, and kitty seized himBefore he'd time to blink;"Oh," he cried, "I'm sorry,But I didn't think."

PHŒBE CARY

TOM THUMB—I

t	pe	s	rein
humb	ople	uit	s
f	fri	b	thist
ought	ghtened	rought	ledown

In the days of King Arthur, there lived a wise man named Merlin.

He knew all the fairies and where they lived.

Even the fairy queen was a friend of his.

Once, while he was traveling, night overtook him in a deep forest.

He rapped at the door of a small cottage and asked for some food.

Merlin looked so hungry and poor that the farmer and his wife took pity on him.

4

They not only gave him a bowl of milk with some brown bread, but they said he might stay through the night.

Merlin saw that, in spite of their pleasant cottage, both the farmer and his wife were very sad.

"Why are you sad?" asked Merlin.

"You seem to have a good farm, a pleasant cottage, and many things to make you happy."

"Ah!" said the woman, "we are unhappy because we have no child.

I should be the happiest woman in the world if I had a son.

Why, even if he were no bigger than my husband's thumb, we should love him dearly."

"That would be indeed a very strange kind of child," said Merlin, "but I hope you may have your wish."

Now Merlin was on his way to call on the queen of the fairies.

When he came to her castle the next day, he told the fairy queen the wish of the farmer's wife.

The queen of the fairies said, "The good woman shall have her wish. I will give her a son no larger than her husband's thumb."

TOM THUMB—II

Soon after this the good farmer's wife had a son. He was, indeed, just the size of his father's thumb.

People came from far and wide to see the tiny boy.

One day the fairy queen and some other fairies came to see him.

The queen kissed the little boy and named him Tom Thumb.

Each of the other fairies made Tom a gift.

He had a shirt made of silk from a spider's web, a coat of thistledown, a hat made from the leaf of an oak, tiny shoes made from a mouse's skin, and many other gifts besides.

Tom never grew any larger than a man's thumb, but he could do many clever tricks.

One day his mother was mixing a pudding.

Tom leaned over the edge of the bowl to see how it was made.

He slipped, and in he went, head first.

His mother did not see him fall, and kept stirring and stirring the pudding.

Tom could not see nor hear, but he kicked and kicked inside the pudding.

The pudding moved and tossed about.

His mother was afraid.

She did not know what to think.

"There must be witches in it," she said.

She went to the window to throw the pudding out.

Just then a poor beggar was passing by the house.

"Here is a pudding you may have, if you like," said Tom's mother.

The beggar thanked her and put it into his basket.

He had not gone very far, when Tom got his head out of the pudding and shouted in a shrill voice:

"Take me out! take me out!"

The poor beggar was so frightened that he dropped his basket, pudding and all, and ran off as fast as he could.

Tom crawled out of the pudding, climbed out of the basket, and ran home.

His mother washed him and put him to bed.

TOM THUMB—III

Not long after this Tom's mother took him with her when she went to milk the cow.

That he might not get lost, she tied him to a wisp of hay.

When Tom's mother was not looking, the cow took the wisp of hay into her mouth.

She began to chew and chew.

Tom began to jump about and shout.

He frightened the cow so that she opened her great mouth and out Tom jumped.

5

Then Tom's mother took him in her apron and ran with him to the house, but he was not hurt in the least.

One day Tom was in the field helping his father.
"Let me drive the horse home," said Tom "You drive the horse!" said his father.
"How could you hold the reins?"
"I could stand in the horse's ear and tell him which way to go," said Tom.
So his father put him in the horse's ear, and he drove safely home.
"Mother! mother!" cried Tom.
But when Tom's mother came out, she could see no one.
She began to be afraid.
"Where are you, Tom?" she cried.
"Here I am in the horse's ear. Please take me down," said Tom.
His mother lifted him gently down, kissed him, and gave him a blackberry for his supper.
Tom's father made him a whip out of a straw.
Tom tried to drive the cows, but he fell into a deep ditch.
There a great bird saw him and thought he was a mouse.
The bird seized Tom in her claws and carried him toward her nest.
As they were passing over the sea, Tom got away and fell into the water, where a great fish swallowed him at one mouthful.
Soon after this the fish was caught, and it was such a big one that it was sent at once to King Arthur.
When the cook cut open the fish, out jumped Tom Thumb. Tom was brought before the king, and his story was told.

TOM THUMB—IV

The king grew very fond of Tom and his wise sayings. He took Tom with him wherever he went.
If it began to rain, Tom would creep into the king's pocket and sleep until the rain was over.
The king had a new suit made for Tom, and gave him a needle for a sword.
A mouse was trained for Tom to ride.
The king and queen never tired of seeing him ride his queer little horse and bravely wave his sword.
One day, as they were going hunting, a cat jumped out and caught Tom's mouse.

Tom drew his sword and tried to drive the cat away.
The king ran to help poor Tom, but the little mouse was dead, and Tom was scratched and bitten.
Tom was put to bed, but he did not die.
No indeed! he was soon well again, and fought many brave battles and did many brave deeds to please the king.

English Fairy Tale

SUPPOSE

w	p	e	
ouldn't	ouring	arnest	ady

Suppose, my little lady,Your doll should break her head,Could you make it whole by cryingTill your eyes and nose are red?And wouldn't it be better farTo treat it as a joke,And say you're glad 'twas Dolly's,And not your head that broke?

Suppose you're dressed for walking,And the rain comes pouring down,Will it clear off any soonerBecause you scold and frown?And wouldn't it be nicerFor you to smile than pout,And so make sunshine in the houseWhen there is none without?

Suppose your task, my little man,Is very hard to get,Will it make it any easierFor you to sit and fret?And wouldn't it be wiserThan waiting like a dunce,To go to work in earnest,And learn the thing at once?

ALICE CARY

CINDERELLA—I

Once upon a time there lived a maiden named Cinderella.

Her mother was dead, and she had to work very, very hard in the kitchen.

She had two older sisters, but they were cross to little Cinderella.

They made her stay among the pots and the kettles and do all the hard work about the house.

Sometimes, to keep warm, she crept in among the cinders.

That is why she was called Cinderella.

One day the sisters came dancing into the house. "We have been invited to the king's ball," they cried.

At length the day of the great ball came, and the two sisters rode away in their fine silk dresses.

Poor Cinderella, who had to stay behind, looked at her old ragged clothes, and burst into tears.

"Alas," she cried, "why should I always have to stay in the kitchen while my sisters dress in silks and satins?"

Hardly had she spoken when there stood before her a dear little old lady with a golden wand in her hand.

"My child," she cried, "I am your fairy godmother, and you shall go to the ball, too.

First go into the garden, Cinderella, and bring to me the largest pumpkin you can find."

When Cinderella had done this, the fairy waved her golden wand over the yellow pumpkin.

In a flash, it was not a pumpkin at all, but a beautiful yellow coach.

"Now bring me four white mice, two large ones and two small ones."

In a moment Cinderella brought a trap full of mice into the room.

The fairy waved her golden wand, and the two largest mice were turned into two snow-white horses.

Two small mice became two men, one a coachman, the other a footman.

"But how am I to go in these clothes?" said Cinderella.

"Ah, let me see," said the fairy, and she slowly waved her wand over the maiden's head.

Oh, what a change!

The rags tumbled to the floor.

And, what do you think! in their place was a beautiful pink silk dress.

The ugly shoes fell off.

And, lo! a tiny pair of glass slippers were on Cinderella's little feet.

"Now listen to what I say," said the fairy godmother. "You must not stay after the clock strikes twelve.

At that time your coach will again be a pumpkin, the men will be mice, and you will have on your old ragged dress."

Cinderella said she would not forget.

Then she jumped into the coach, and away she drove to the king's ball.

CINDERELLA—II

The king's son was charmed with Cinderella.

She was so very beautiful that he would dance with her and with no one else.

Cinderella had such a good time that she forgot about the clock.

It began to strike twelve—one, two, three.

Cinderella ran from the room.

7

Down the steps of the palace she flew.

She ran so fast that she lost one of her little glass slippers.

The clock finished striking.

Lo! the coach turned into a pumpkin.

The horses and men turned into mice.

Poor Cinderella had to walk home in her ragged clothes.

The next morning the prince found Cinderella's little glass slipper on the stairs.

"There is only one maiden in all the world who can wear so tiny a slipper," said the prince. "I will marry her and no other."

The prince hunted far and wide for a maiden who could put it on. Many tried, but none could do it.

At last he came to the house where Cinderella lived. The two older sisters tried and tried to put the slipper on their large feet.

While the prince was waiting, Cinderella came into the room.

"Let me try it," she said.

"You!" cried the older sisters. "You could never put it on."

"Let her try it," said the prince.

At once the little glass slipper was fitted to the tiny foot.

Then Cinderella stood up; her ragged clothes turned into a beautiful silk dress, and there were two little slippers on her two little feet.

Then the prince knew that Cinderella was the one he had danced with at the ball, and taking her hand, he led her out to his coach.

Soon they were married and lived happily ever after.

English Fairy Tale

RAINDROPS

Oh, where do you come from,You little drops of rain,Pitter-patter, pitter-patter,Down the windowpane?

Tell me, little raindrops,Is that the way you play?Pitter-patter, pitter-patter,All the rainy day?

I sit here at the window;I've nothing else to do;Oh, I wish that I could play,This rainy day, with you!

The little raindrops cannot speak,But "pitter-patter-pat"Means, "We can play on this side,Why can't you play on that?"

ANN HAWKSHAWE

THE FOUR FRIENDS—I

omb	usic	iants	hief

Once upon a time a man had a donkey.

His donkey had worked for him many years.

At last the donkey grew so old that he was no longer of any use for work, and his master wished to get rid of him.

The donkey, fearing he might be killed, ran away.

He took the road to Bremen, where he had often heard the street band playing.

He liked music, so he thought he might join the band.

He had not gone far when he came upon an old dog.

The dog was panting, as if he had been running a long way.

"Why are you panting, my friend?" asked the donkey.

"Ah," said the dog, "I am too old for the hunt. My master wished to have me killed. So I ran away. But how I am to find bread and meat, I do not know."

8

"Well," said the donkey, "come with me. I am going to play in the band at Bremen. I think you and I can easily earn a living by music. I can play the lute, and you can play the kettledrum."

The dog was quite willing, and so they be walked on.

They had not gone far when they saw a cat sitting in a yard.

He looked as sad as three days of rainy weather.

"What's the matter with you, old Tom?" asked the donkey.

"You would be sad, too," said the cat, "if you were in my place; for now that I am getting old and cannot catch mice, they wish to drown me. I have run away, but how I am going to live, I do not know."

"Come with us to Bremen," said the donkey. "We are going to play in the band. I know you love music, as you sing so well at night. You too can join the band."

"That is just what I should like to do," said the cat.

So the donkey, the dog, and the cat all walked on together.

After a time the three came to a farmyard.

There on the gate sat a cock, crying "Cock-a-doodle-doo" with all his might.

"Why are you making so much noise?" asked the donkey.

"Ah," said the cock, "I find I must have my head cut off so that I may serve as a dinner for Monday. I'm crowing as hard as I can while my head is still on."

"Come with us, old Red Comb," said the donkey. "We are going to Bremen to join the band. You have a fine voice. You can join, too."

"Ah," said the cock, "that is just what I should like to do."

And they all went on their way to Bremen.

THE FOUR FRIENDS—II

At evening the four friends came to a wood, where they stopped for the night.

The donkey and the dog lay down under a large tree.

The cat climbed up on one of the branches.

The cock flew to the very top of the tree, where he felt quite safe.

From his perch on the top of the tree the cock saw a light.

Calling to his friends, he said, "We are not far from a house. I can see a light."

"Let us go on," said the donkey, "for it may be just the house for us."

As they drew near, the light grew larger and brighter.

At last they could see that it came from the window of a robber's house.

The donkey, who was the tallest, went up and looked in.

"What do you see, old Long Ears?" asked the cock.

"What do I see?" answered the donkey. "Why, a table spread with plenty to eat and drink, and the robbers having their supper."

"We should be there, too, if we had our rights," said the cock.

"Ah, yes," said the donkey; "if we could only get inside."

Then the four friends talked over what they had better do in order to drive the robbers out of the house.

At last they hit upon a plan.

The donkey stood upon his hind legs and placed his front feet on the window sill.

The dog then stood on the donkey's back

The cat climbed upon the dog, while the cock perched upon the cat's head.

The donkey gave a signal, and they began all at the same time, to make their loudest music.

The donkey brayed, the dog barked, the cat mewed, and the cock crowed, all with such force that the windowpane shook and was almost broken.

The robbers had never heard such a noise.

They thought it must come from witches, or giants, or goblins, and they all ran as fast as they could to the wood behind the house.

Then our four friends rushed in and ate what the robbers had left upon the table.

It did not take long, for they acted as if they had been hungry for a month.

When the four had eaten, they put out the light, and each went to sleep in the spot which he liked the best.

The donkey lay down in the yard.

The dog lay behind the door.

The cat curled himself in front of the fire, while the cock flew up on a high beam.

They soon fell fast asleep.

THE FOUR FRIENDS—III

When all was still and the light was out, the robber chief sent one of his bravest men back to the house.

The man found the house quiet, so he went into the kitchen to strike a light.

Seeing the great fiery eyes of the cat, he thought they were live coals and held a match to them.

Puss was so angry that he flew up and scratched the man's face. This gave the robber a great fright, and he ran for the door.

As he went by, the dog sprang up and bit him in the leg.

In the yard the robber ran into the donkey, who gave him a great kick.

The cock on the beam was waked by the! noise, and cried, "Cock-a-doodle-doo!"

The man ran as fast as his legs could carry him back to the robber chief.

"Ah!" he cried. "In that house is a wicked witch, who flew at me and scratched my face with her long nails.

By the door stood a man with a knife, who cut me in the leg.

Out in the yard lay a great black giant, who struck me a blow with his wooden club.

Upon the roof sat the judge, who cried, 'What did he do? What did he do?'

When I heard this I ran off as fast as I could."

The robbers never went near the house again.

The four friends liked the place so well that they would not leave it, and so far as I know, they are there to this day.

WILLIAM AND JACOB GRIMM

LITTLE BIRDIE

What does little birdie say,In her nest at peep of day?Let me fly, says little birdie,Mother, let me fly away.Birdie, rest a little longer,Till the little wings are stronger.So she rests a little longer,Then she flies away.

What does little baby say,In her bed at peep of day?Baby says, like little birdie,Let me rise and fly away.Baby, sleep a little longer,Till the little limbs are stronger.If she sleeps a little longer,Baby too shall fly away.

ALFRED TENNYSON

MOTHER FROST—I

road	da ughters	t hrough	eart

At the edge of a wood there was a great, clear, bubbling spring of cold water.

Near this spring lived a widow and her two daughters.

One of them was very beautiful and a great help about the house, while the other was ugly and idle.

The mother loved only the ugly one, for she was her own child.

She cared so little for the other daughter that she made her do all the hard work.

Every day the poor girl would sit beside the spring and spin and spin, until her fingers bled.

One day, while she was washing the blood from her hands, the spindle fell into the spring and sank to the bottom.

With tears in her eyes, she ran and told her stepmother what she had done.

The stepmother was angry and said, "You let the spindle fall into the spring. Now you must go and get it out."

The maiden went back to the spring to look for the spindle.

She leaned so far over the edge that her hand slipped, and down, down, she sank to the very bottom.

All at once she found that she was in a beautiful field where many wild flowers grew.

As she walked across the field, she came to a baker's oven full of new bread.

The loaves cried to her, "Oh, pull us out! pull us out, or we shall burn!"

"Indeed I will!" cried the maiden.

Stepping up, she pulled all the sweet brown loaves out of the oven.

As she walked along, she came to a tree full of apples.

The tree cried, "Shake me! shake me! my apples are all quite ripe!"

"Indeed I will!" cried the maiden.

So she shook the tree again and again, until there was not an apple left on its branches.

Then she picked up the apples, one by one, and piled them in a great heap.

When she had picked up all the apples, she walked on.

At last she came to a small house.

In the doorway sat an old woman who had such large teeth that the girl felt afraid of her and turned to run away.

Then the old woman cried, "What do you fear, my child? Come in and live here with me. If you will do the work about the house, I will be very kind to you. Only take care to make my bed well.

You must shake it and pound it so that the feathers will fly about. Then the children down on the earth will say that snowflakes are falling, for I am Mother Frost."

The old woman spoke so kindly that she won the maiden's heart.

"I will gladly work for you," she said.

The girl did her work well, and each day she shook up the bed until the feathers flew about like snowflakes.

She was very happy with Mother Frost, who never spoke an angry word.

After the girl had stayed a long time with the kind old woman, she began to feel homesick.

She could not help it, though her life with Mother Frost had been so happy.

At length she said, "Dear Mother Frost, you have been very kind to me, but I should like to go home to my friends."

"I am pleased to hear you say that you wish to go home," said Mother Frost. "You have worked for me so well that I will show you the way myself."

She took the maiden by the hand and led her to a broad gateway.

The gate was open, and as she went through a shower of gold fell over the maiden.

It clung to her clothes, so that she was dressed in gold from her head to her feet.

"That is your pay for having worked so hard," said the old woman. "And here is your spindle that fell into the spring."

Then the gate was closed, and the maiden found herself once more in the world.

She was not far from her own home, and as she came into the farmyard, a cock on the roof cried loudly:

"Cock-a-doodle-doo!

Our golden lady has come home, too."

MOTHER FROST—II

When the stepmother saw the girl with her golden dress, she was kind to her. Then the maiden told how the gold had fallen upon her.

The mother could hardly wait to have her own child try her luck in the same way.

This time she made the idle daughter go to the spring and spin.

The lazy girl did not spin fast enough to make her fingers bleed.

So she pricked her finger with a thorn until a few drops of blood stained the spindle.

At once she let it drop into the water, and sprang in after it herself.

11

The ugly girl found herself in a beautiful field, just as her sister had.
She walked along the same path until she came to the baker's oven.
She heard the loaves cry, "Pull us out! pull us out, or we shall burn!"

But the lazy girl said to the brown loaves, "I will not. I do not want to soil my hands in your dirty oven."
Then she walked on until she came to the apple tree.
"Shake me! shake me!" it cried, "for my apples are quite ripe."
"I will not," said the girl, "for some of your apples might fall on my head."
As she spoke, she walked lazily on.
At last the girl stood before the door of Mother Frost's house.
She had no fear of Mother Frost's great teeth, but walked right up to the old woman and offered to be her servant.
For a whole day the girl was very busy, and did everything that she was told to do.
On the second day she began to be lazy, and on the third day she was still worse.
She would not get up in the morning.
The bed was never made, or shaken, so the feathers could fly about.
At last Mother Frost grew tired of her and told her that she must go away.
This was what the lazy girl wanted, for she felt sure that now she would have the golden shower.
Mother Frost led her to the great gate, but she passed under it, a kettle full of black pitch was upset over her.

"That is what you get for your work," said the old woman, as she shut the gate.
The idle girl walked home, covered with pitch.
When she went into the farmyard the cock on the roof cried out:
"Cock-a-doodle-doo!
Our sticky lady has come home, too."
The pitch stuck so fast to the girl that, as long as she lived, it never came off.

WILLIAM AND JACOB GRIMM

IF EVER I SEE

If ever I see,On bush or tree,Young birds in their pretty nest;I must not, in play,Steal the birds away,To grieve their mother's breast.

My mother, I know,Would sorrow so,Should I be stolen away;So I'll speak to the birdsIn my softest words,Nor hurt them in my play.

And when they can flyIn the bright blue sky,They'll warble a song to me;And then if I'm sadIt will make me gladTo think they are happy and free.

LYDIA MARIA CHILD

WHY THE BEAR'S TAIL IS SHORT

Did you ever go to a circus where there was a bear in a cage?
Did you notice how short his tail was?
I will tell you how the bear's tail came to be short.
One very cold day in winter, a fox saw some men taking home a load of fish.
The fox jumped upon the wagon while the men were not looking.
He threw off some of the best fish until he had enough for his dinner.
Then Mr. Fox jumped from the wagon and began to eat the fish.
While he was eating the fish, Mr. Bear came along.
"Good morning," said Mr. Bear, "you have had good luck fishing to-day. Those are very fine fish. How did you catch them?"
"They are fine fish," said Mr. Fox.
"If you will go fishing with me to-night, I will show you how to catch even better fish than these."
"I will go with you gladly," said the bear. "I will bring my hook and line too."

"You don't need a hook and line," said the fox.

"I always catch fish with my tail. You have a much longer tail than I, and can fish so much the better."

At sunset the bear met the fox.

They went across the frozen river until they came to a small hole in the ice.

"Now, Mr. Bear," said the fox, "sit down here on the ice and put your tail through the hole. You must keep still for a long while. That is the best way to catch fish.

Wait until a great many fish take hold of your tail. Then pull with all your might."

The bear sat very still for a long time.

At last he began to feel cold and he moved a little.

"Ow!" he cried, for his tail had begun freeze in the ice.

"Is it not time to pull out the fish?" said the bear.

"No, no," cried the fox.

"Wait until more fish have taken hold of your tail. You are very strong. You can wait a little longer."

So the poor bear waited until it was almost morning.

Just then some dogs began to bark on the bank of the river.

The bear was so afraid that he jumped up quickly and pulled with all his might, but his tail was frozen fast in the ice.

He pulled and pulled until at length the tail was broken short off.

Mr. Fox ran away laughing and laughing at the trick he had played upon Mr. Bear.

Bears' tails have been short ever since.

German Folk Tale

RUMPELSTILTSKIN—I

gl istened	uess	ŋ ourn	c hamber

Once upon a time there lived a miller who had a beautiful daughter.

Now the miller had to visit the king's castle and, while there, he happened to meet the king face to face.

The king stopped and spoke to the miller. The miller, wishing the king to think that he was very rich, told him that he had a daughter who could spin straw into gold.

"Ah," said the king, "that is indeed a wonderful gift. To-morrow you must bring your daughter to my castle, that she may spin some gold for me."

Then the miller was afraid and wished he had not spoken, but he had to do as the king ordered.

The next day he brought his daughter to the castle.

Now it happened that the king loved gold above all things. So taking the poor girl by the hand, he led her into one of the great rooms of the castle.

There, in the middle of the room, stood a spinning wheel, and near it was a great heap of straw.

The king turned to the miller's daughter, and said:

"There is your spinning wheel, and here is the straw. If you do not spin all of it into gold by morning, your head shall be cut off."

Then the king left the room and locked the door behind him.

The poor girl could only sit and weep, for she had not the least idea how to spin straw into gold.

While she was crying, the door flew open and a little old man stepped into the room.

He had bandy legs, a long red nose, and wore a tall, peaked cap. Bowing low to the maiden he said:

"Good evening, my dear young lady. Why are you crying?"

"Alas," said the girl, "the king has ordered me to spin all this straw into gold, and I do not know how."

Then the little man said, "What will you give me if I will spin it for you?"

"This string of gold beads from my neck," said the girl.

The little man took the beads, and, sitting down, began to spin.

Whir! whir! went the wheel; round and round it whirled.

Lo, as the maiden looked, she saw the coarse straw turn into beautiful golden threads.

The little man kept so busily at work that soon all the straw was gone, and in its place lay a heap of the finest gold.

The next morning the king unlocked the door. How his eyes sparkled at the sight of the gold!

These riches made the king even more greedy than before.

He led the maiden to a still larger chamber, which was full of straw.

Turning to the trembling girl, he said, "There is your spinning wheel, and here is the straw. If you do not spin all of it into gold by morning, your head shall be cut off."

The maiden's eyes filled with tears at the sight of that huge heap of straw. Sitting down, she began to cry.

All at once the door opened and in jumped the little old man. He took off his pointed cap and said to the miller's daughter, "What will you give me if I help you again, and spin this straw into gold?"

"This ring from my finger," said the maiden.

The little man took the ring, and seating himself before the spinning wheel, began to spin.

Whir! whir! went the wheel. Faster and faster it whirled.

In the morning the straw had all been turned into finest gold.

When the king opened the door, how his eyes glistened at the sight of the gold! Still, it only made him greedy for more, so taking the poor girl by the hand, he led her to a much larger chamber.

This was so full of straw that there was hardly room for her to sit at the spinning wheel.

Turning to the maiden, the king said:

"There is your spinning wheel, and here is the straw. If you do not spin all of it into gold by morning, your head shall be cut off. But if you do spin the gold, I will marry you and make you my queen."

"For," thought the king, "though she is only a miller's daughter, yet she can make me the richest king in the world."

Hardly had the door closed behind the king, when the little old man came hopping and skipping into the room.

Taking off his pointed cap, he said to the girl, "What will you give me if I will again spin this straw for you?"

"Ah!" said the maiden, "I have nothing more to give."

"Then you must make me a promise," said the little man. "You must promise to give me your first child, after you have become queen."

The poor girl saw no other way to save her life, so she gave her promise to the little man.

Then he sat down and began to spin.

Whir! whir! went the wheel. Faster and faster he spun.

Soon the great roomful of straw was all turned into gold.

When the king opened the door the next morning, he saw the maiden sitting beside a large heap of shining gold.

The king kept his promise, and made the poor miller's daughter his queen.

RUMPELSTILTSKIN—II

About a year later the queen had a lovely child, but she forgot all about her promise.

One day the little old man came hopping into the queen's room and said, "Now give me what you have promised."

The queen was filled with terror, and offered the little man all the riches of the kingdom if he would leave her the child.

"No, I do not care for riches; you must keep your promise."

Then the queen began to mourn and to weep, until the little man had pity for her.

"I will give you three days," he said, "and if, in that time, you can guess my name, you shall keep the child."

The queen lay awake that night, thinking of all the names she had ever heard. In the morning men were sent to every part of the kingdom to find strange names.

The next day the little man came again. The queen began to call off to him all the names that she had found—Caspar, Melchior, and many, many others.

At each one the little man shook his head, and said, "No, that is not my name."

Then the queen had her men go from house to house through the town. They took down the name of every man, woman, and child.

When the little man came again, the queen had a long list of names to give him.

"Is your name Cowribs, or Sheepshanks, or Bandy legs?" she said to him at last.

He answered to each one, "No, that is not my name."

On the third day the queen's men began to come back from all parts of the kingdom. They had been far and wide to find new names.

One of these men said, "I could not find any new names, but going by some deep woods, I heard a fox wish good-night to a rabbit.

Soon I came upon a little house, in front of which a fire was burning. Around this fire danced a little man. He wore a pointed cap, and had a long nose and bandy legs. As he went hopping and jumping about, first on one leg and then on the other, he sang:

My baking and brewing I will do to-day,The queen's son to-morrow I will take away,No wise man can show the queen where to begin,For my name, to be sure, is Rumpelstiltskin."

The queen clapped her hands for joy. She knew that at last she had found the name.

She sent the servant away with a bag of gold, and waited for the queer little man to come to her. At sunset the little fellow came hopping and skipping up to the queen.

"Now, O queen," he said, "this is your last chance. Tell me my name."

The queen asked, "Is your name Conrad?"

"No."

"Henry?"

"No."

"Then your name is Rumpelstiltskin."

"The fairies have told you!" shouted the little man dancing about.

He became so angry that, in his rage, he stamped his right foot into the ground.

This made him more angry still, and taking hold of his left foot with both hands, he pulled so hard that he tore himself quite in two.

WILLIAM AND JACOB GRIMM

BED IN SUMMER

In winter I get up at nightAnd dress by yellow candle-light.In summer, quite the other way,I have to go to bed by day.

I have to go to bed and seeThe birds still hopping on the tree,Or hear the grown-up people's feetStill going past me in the street.

And does it not seem hard to you,When all the sky is clear and blue,And I should like so much to play,To have to go to bed by day?

ROBERT LOUIS STEVENSON

THE GOLDEN TOUCH—I

ouch	s lightest	c reature	tatue

Many years ago there lived a king named Midas.

King Midas had one little daughter, whose name was Marigold.

King Midas was very, very rich. It was said that he had more gold than any other king in the world.

One room of his great castle was almost filled with yellow gold pieces.

At last the king grew so fond of his gold that he loved it better than anything else in all the world.

He even loved it better than his own little daughter, dear little rosy-cheeked Marigold. His one great wish seemed to be for more and more gold.

One day while he was in his gold room counting his money, a beautiful fairy boy stood before him.

The boy's face shone with a wonderful light, and he had wings on his cap and wings on his feet. In his hand he carried a strange-looking wand, and the wand also had wings.

"Midas, you are the richest man in the world," said the fairy. "There is no king who has so much gold as you."

"That may be," said the king. "As you see, I have this room full of gold, but I should like much more; for gold is the best and the most wonderful thing in the world."

"Are you sure?" asked the fairy.

"I am very sure," answered the king.

"If I should grant you one wish," said the fairy, "would you ask for more gold?"

"If I could have but one wish," said the king, "I would ask that everything I touched should turn to beautiful yellow gold."

"Your wish shall be granted," said the fairy "At sunrise to-morrow morning your slightest touch will turn everything into gold. But warn you that your gift will not make you happy."

"I will take the risk," said the king.

THE GOLDEN TOUCH—II

The next morning King Midas awoke very early. He was eager to see if the fairy's promise had come true.

As soon as the sun arose he tried the gift by touching the bed lightly with his hand.

The bed turned to gold.

He touched the chair and table.

Upon the instant they were turned to solid gold.

The king was wild with joy.

He ran around the room, touching everything he could see. His magic gift turned all to shining, yellow gold.

The king soon felt hungry and went down to eat his breakfast. Now a strange thing happened. When he raised a glass of clear cold water to drink, it became solid gold.

Not a drop of water could pass his lips.

The bread turned to gold under his fingers.

The meat was hard, and yellow, and shiny.

Not a thing could he get to eat.

All was gold, gold, gold.

His little daughter came running in from the garden.

Of all living creatures she was the dearest to him.

He touched her hair with his lips.

At once the little girl was changed to a golden statue.

A great fear crept into the king's heart, sweeping all the joy out of his life.

In his grief he called and called upon the fairy who had given him the gift of the golden touch.

16

"O fairy," he begged, "take away this horrible golden gift! Take all my lands. Take all my gold. Take everything, only give me back my little daughter."

In a moment the beautiful fairy was standing before him.

"Do you still think that gold is the greatest thing in the world?" asked the fairy.

"No! no!" cried the king. "I hate the very sight of the yellow stuff."

"Are you sure that you no longer wish the golden touch?" asked the fairy.

"I have learned my lesson," said the king. "I no longer think gold the greatest thing in the world."

"Very well," said the fairy, "take this pitcher to the spring in the garden and fill it with water. Then sprinkle those things which you have touched and turned to gold."

The king took the pitcher and rushed to the spring. Running back, he first sprinkled the head of his dear little girl. Instantly she became his own darling Marigold again, and gave him a kiss.

The king sprinkled the golden food, and to his great joy it turned back to real bread and real butter.

Then he and his little daughter sat down to breakfast. How good the cold water tasted. How eagerly the hungry king ate the bread and butter, the meat, and all the good food.

The king hated his golden touch so much that he sprinkled even the chairs and the tables and everything else that the fairy's gift had turned to gold.

Greek Myth

OVER IN THE MEADOW

Over in the meadow,In the sand, in the sun,Lived an old mother toadAnd her little toadie one."Wink!" said the mother;"I wink," said the one;So she winked and she blinkedIn the sand, in the sun.

Over in the meadow,Where the stream runs blue,Lived an old mother fishAnd her little fishes two."Swim!" said the mother;"We swim," said the two;So they swam and they leapedWhere the stream runs blue.

Over in the meadow,In a hole in a tree,Lived a mother bluebirdAnd her little birdies three."Sing!" said the mother;"We sing," said the three;So they sang and were gladIn the hole in the tree.

Over in the meadow,In a snug beehive,Lived a mother honeybeeAnd her little honeys five."Buzz!" said the mother;"We buzz," said the five;So they buzzed and they hummedIn the snug beehive.

Over in the meadow,Where the clear pools shine,Lived a green mother frog,And her little froggies nine."Croak!" said the mother;"We croak," said the nine;So they croaked and they splashedWhere the clear pools shine.

Over in the meadow,In a sly little den,Lived a gray mother spiderAnd her little spiders ten."Spin!" said the mother;"We spin," said the ten;So they spun lace websIn their sly little den.

OLIVE A. WADSWORTH

THE BELL OF ATRI

iser	ustice	hose

Once upon a time a good and wise king ruled in the city of Atri.

He wished all his people to be happy.

In order that justice might be done to every one, he ordered a great bell to be hung in a tower.

Tied to the bell was a strong rope, so long that it reached nearly to the ground.

"I have placed the bell in the center of my city," said the king, "so that it will be near all the people. The rope I have made long, so that even a little child can reach it."

Then the king gave out this order:

"If there be any one among my people who feels that he has not been justly treated, let him ring this bell.

Then, whether he be old or young, rich or poor, his story shall be heard."

The bell of justice had hung in its place for many years.

Many times it had been rung by the poor and needy, and justice had been done.

At length the old rope became worn with use and age.

When it was taken down, another rope, long enough and strong enough, could not be found. So the king had to send away for one.

"What if some one should need help while the rope is down?" cried the people. "We must find something to take its place."

So one of the men cut a long grapevine and fastened it to the great bell.

It was in the springtime, and green shoots and leaves hung from the grapevine rope.

Near Atri, there lived a rich old soldier.

This soldier owned a horse that had been with him through many battles.

The horse had grown old and lame, and was no longer able to work.

So his cruel master turned him out into the streets to get his living as best he could.

"If you cannot find enough to eat, then you may die," said the miser; "you are of no use to me."

The old horse went limping along; he grew thinner and thinner.

At length he limped up to the tower where the bell of justice hung.

His dim eyes saw the green shoots and the fresh leaves of the grapevine.

Thinking they were good to eat, he gave a pull at the vine.

"Ding-dong! ding-dong!" said the great bell. The people came running from all sides.

"Who is calling for justice?" they cried.

There stood the old horse, chewing on the grapevine.

"Ding-dong! ding-dong!" rang the great bell.

"Whose horse is this?" asked the judges, as they came running up.

Then the story of the old horse was told.

The judges sent for his cruel master.

They ordered that he should build a warm barn, and that the faithful horse should have the best of hay and grain as long as he lived.

The people shouted for joy at this act of justice, but the miser hung his head in shame and led the old horse away.

German Folk Tale

THE BABY

No shoes to hide her tiny toes,No stockings on her feet;Her little ankles white as snow,Or early blossoms sweet.

Her simple dress of sprinkled pink;Her tiny, dimpled chin;Her rosebud lips and bonny mouthWith not one tooth between.

Her eyes so like her mother's own,Two gentle, liquid things;Her face is like an angel's face—We're glad she has no wings.

HUGH MILLER

BRUCE AND THE SPIDER

Robert Bruce, King of Scotland, was hiding in a hut in the forest. His enemies were seeking him far and wide.

Six times he had met them in battle, and six times he had failed. Hope and courage were gone.

Bruce had given up all as lost. He was about to run away from Scotland, and to leave the country in the hands of his enemies.

Full of sorrow, he lay stretched on a pile of straw in the poor woodchopper's hut. While he lay thinking, he noticed a spider spinning her web.

The spider was trying to spin a thread from one beam of the cottage to another. It was a long way between the beams, and Bruce saw how hard a thing it was for her to do.

"She can never do it," thought the king.

The little spider tried it once and failed She tried it twice and failed. The king counted each time. At length she had tried it six times and had failed each time.

"She is like me," thought the king. "I have tried six battles and failed. She has tried six times to reach the beam and failed."

Then starting up from the straw, he cried, "I will hang my fate upon that little spider.

If she swings the seventh time and fails, then I will give up all for lost. If she swings the seventh time and wins, I will call my men together once more for a battle with the enemy."

The spider tried the seventh time, letting herself down upon her slender thread. She swung out bravely.

"Look! look!" shouted the king. "She has reached it. The thread hangs between the two beams. If the spider can do it, I can do it."

Bruce got up from the straw with new strength and sent his men from village to village, calling the people to arms.

The brave soldiers answered his call and came trooping in.

At length his army was ready to fight, and when the king led them in a great battle against the enemy, this time, like the spider, Bruce won.

Scottish Tradition

THE WISE LITTLE PIG

Where are you going, you little pig?"I'm leaving my mother, I'm growing so big."So big, young pig!So young, so big!What! leaving your mother, you foolish young pig?

Where are you going, you little pig?"I've got a new spade, and I'm going to dig."To dig, little pig!A little pig dig!Well, I never saw a pig with a spade, that could dig!

Where are you going, you little pig?"I'm going to have a nice ride in a gig."In a gig, little pig!What! a pig in a gig!Well, I never yet saw a pig ride in a gig!

Where are you going, you little pig?"I'm going to the barber's to buy me a wig."A wig, little pig!A pig in a wig!Why, whoever before saw a pig in a wig?

Where are you going, you little pig?"I'm going to the ball to dance a fine jig."A jig, little pig!A pig dance a jig!Well, I never before saw a pig dance a jig!

ANONYMOUS

AN INDIAN STORY—I

b	tom		t
elieve	ahawks	igns	ongue

Many years ago two boys lived on a farm in New England.

It was so long ago that there were few white people in this country.

The farms were scattered, and around them were great forests.

The houses were made of logs, with strong, heavy doors.

Far away in the woods lived many Indians.

Sometimes the Indians would come down where the white people lived, and would capture any white person whom they could find.

They even dared to attack, and often burned, the scattered log cabins.

The white prisoners would be taken to the Indian villages and would be held there as captives.

One cold winter morning the two brothers, John and William, were going skating on the river.

In order to reach the river, they had to pass through some woods.

John, the older brother, started first.

He threw his skates over his back and ran off whistling toward the river.

William, the younger brother, had to stay behind to fill with wood the huge box beside the fireplace.

Indians had not been seen near the farm for many years, so John was not in the least afraid.

As he went through the woods toward the river two huge Indians, with painted faces, jumped from behind the trees where they had been hiding.

Before John could run he was caught, and his hands were tied behind his back.

Then they heard William shout as he ran down the path after his brother.

John knew that the Indians might kill him if he warned his brother.

But he was brave, and before they could stop him, he cried out, "Indians! Indians!"

The Indians were angry and struck at John with their tomahawks.

But he was not afraid; he faced the Indians bravely.

William heard the shout of warning, and ran like a deer back to the log cabin.

The heavy door was shut with a slam, and John's father, with his rifle, waited for the Indian attack.

But the two Indians did not dare attack the log cabin.

Dragging John after them, they started up the river bank toward their Indian town, many, many miles away.

All day long they traveled, and at night they built a small fire.

Over this fire they roasted a partridge which one of them had shot. John was given his share of the bird and a handful of parched Indian corn.

The Indians looked at John's skates, which still hung over his shoulder.

They did not know what skates were. They thought they must be some of the white man's magic.

On and on they traveled for many days, following an old Indian path.

All through the long march John still carried his skates.

At length they came to the Indian village.

AN INDIAN STORY—II

The Indian houses were long huts covered with strips of birch bark.

Four or five families lived in each of these houses.

John was given to an Indian woman who had lost her own boy the year before.

John's Indian mother was good to him, and treated him as if he were her own son.

One time the Indian boys thought they would test John's courage, so they formed in two lines, while each boy held a stout stick.

Then they ordered John to run down between the two long lines.

They had their sticks all ready to beat him.

They thought John would be afraid and so would do as they told him.

But John was a strong lad, and jumping upon the first Indian boy, he took his stick away from him.

Armed with this stick, John struck right and left at the heads of the boys until they were all glad to run away.

The Indian men liked to see John's courage, and laughed long and loud when the Indian boys ran away.

After this the boys were glad to have John play with them.

With their bows and arrows they shot at a mark.

They swam in the river and played games of tag, hide and seek, and ball.

In the spring the Indian women planted the yellow corn.

When the corn was up, the squaws went into the fields to hoe out the weeds. For a hoe they used a flat piece of stone tied to a wooden handle.

As John was a white boy the squaws tried to make him help hoe the corn.

When John took the hoe, he hoed up the corn and left the weeds.

The angry squaws made signs to him that he must not do so.

Then John threw the hoe far from him.

"Hoeing is fit for squaws, not for warriors," he shouted. He had learned this from the Indian boys.

The old men were pleased. They thought John would make a fine warrior.

AN INDIAN STORY—III

John had lived with the Indians a year.

He had learned to speak their tongue, but they did not trust him.

Some of them were always with him, for they were afraid he would run away.

All this time John had kept his skates carefully hidden.

One day the ice froze clear and smooth. John brought his skates down to the river bank.

Many of the Indians followed to see what he was going to do.

They crowded around him on the ice.

John thought he would play a trick on them.

He strapped the skates upon the feet of an Indian boy.

The boy tried to stand up, but his feet slipped out from under him, and down he bumped upon the ice.

How the Indians laughed!

They thought it was a great joke.

Each of them in turn tried on the skates.

How they sprawled and fell upon the ice!

What fun it was for the other Indians!

When they were tired of the sport they held out the skates to John and asked him to put them on.

John strapped on the skates with great care. He was a good skater, but he made believe that he could not skate at all.

He fell down and bumped his head.

He tripped over his toes and made great fun for the Indians.

They did not see that each time he fell he was a little farther out on the ice.

All at once John jumped up.

Away he flew, skating for his life.

Down the river he went, swift as a bird.

The Indians rushed after him, but he had too great a start.

The Indians were swift runners, but John, on his skates, was swifter still.

He knew that the river must flow toward the ocean, and that near the ocean lived the white people.

On and on he skated.

Two days later he saw the smoke of a white man's cabin and knew that he was safe.

John soon found his father and mother.

How glad they were to see him!

A GOOD PLAY

We built a ship upon the stairs,All made of the back-bedroom chairs,And filled it full of sofa pillows,To go a-sailing on the billows.

We took a saw and several nails,And water in the nursery pails;And Tom said, "Let us also takeAn apple and a slice of cake,"—Which was enough for Tom and meTo go a-sailing on, till tea.

We sailed along for days and days,And had the very best of plays;But Tom fell out and hurt his knee,So there was no one left but me.

ROBERT LOUIS STEVENSON

DICK WHITTINGTON—I

Dick Whittington was a poor little boy who lived in the country.

His father and mother were both dead.

Poor little Dick was always willing to work, but sometimes there was no work for him to do, so he often had nothing to eat.

Now Dick was a bright boy.

He kept both ears open to hear what was said around him.

He had heard many times about the great city of London.

Men said that in this great city the people were rich.

Dick had even heard that the streets were paved with gold.

"How I should like to visit that great city," thought Dick, "for I could pick up gold from the streets!"

Dick had earned a little money, so one day he set out to walk to London.

He walked and walked and walked, but London was a long way from his home.

At last a man with a wagon came along. He was a kind man, and he gave Dick a ride.

"Where are you going?" asked Dick.

"I'm going to London," said the man.

"You are very good to give me a ride. I am going there, too," said Dick.

It was dark when they reached London.

That night Dick slept in a barn with the horses.

The next morning he looked for the golden stones in the streets.

He looked and looked, but he could find only dust and dirt.

There were many, many people in London, and Dick thought that he could soon find something to do.

He wandered around the streets, seeking for work.

He asked many people, but no one wanted the poor little country boy.

As Dick had no money for food, he soon became very, very hungry.

At last he grew so weak that he fell down before the door of a great house.

Here the cook found him and began to beat him with a stick.

"Run away, you lazy boy!" she cried.

Poor Dick tried to rise, but he was so faint from want of food that he could not stand.

Just then the owner of the house, Mr. Fitzwarren, came up. He took pity on the poor boy and ordered the cook to give him some food.

Then he turned to Dick and said:

"If you wish to work, you may help the cook in the kitchen. You will find a bed in the attic."

Dick thanked Mr. Fitzwarren again and again for his kindness.

The cook was very cross to Dick and whipped him almost every day.

His bed in the attic was only a pile of old rags.

He soon found that there were many rats and mice in the attic.

They ran over his bed and made so much noise every night that he could not sleep.

"I wish I had a cat," thought Dick, "for she could eat up these rats and mice."

One day Dick earned a penny by blacking a man's shoes.

"I will try to buy a cat with this penny," thought Dick.

So he started out and soon met a woman with a large cat.

"Will you sell me that cat?" said Dick. "I will give you this penny for her."

"You are a good boy," said the woman, "and you may have the cat for a penny, for I know you will treat her kindly."

That night Dick's bed was free from rats, and Miss Puss had a good supper.

Dick began to love his cat dearly.

DICK WHITTINGTON—II

Now Mr. Fitzwarren had many ships which sailed to distant lands.

When a ship sailed Mr. Fitzwarren let every one in his house send something on it.

The things were sold, and when the ship came back, each person had the money for what he had sent.

One of the ships was ready to sail.

Every one in the house except Dick had sent something.

"What is Dick going to send in the ship?" said Mr. Fitzwarren.

"Oh, that boy has nothing to send," said the cross cook.

"It is true," said poor Dick; "I have nothing but my dear cat."

"Well, then you must send your cat," said Mr. Fitzwarren.

How lonely poor Dick was without Puss!

The cook made fun of him for sending a cat on the ship.

At last Dick became so unhappy that he made up his mind to run away.

He started early in the morning, before any one in the house was up.

He had gone but a short way when he heard the sound of the six great bells of Bow.

As they rang, "Ding-dong, ding-dong!" they seemed to say:

Turn back, Whittington,Lord Mayor of London.

"It is strange that the bells should speak to me," said Dick, "but if I am to be Lord Mayor of London, I will gladly turn back."

So he ran back to the house of Mr. Fitzwarren.

"I hope they have not missed me," said Dick, as he gently opened the door and stole softly in.

DICK WHITTINGTON—III

Dick's cat was taken across the ocean. The ship sailed and sailed, until at last it came to a distant country.

Now the king and queen of this country were very rich. When the captain was asked to show his goods before them he was very glad indeed to do so.

The king and queen first gave the captain a great feast.

Gold and silver dishes filled with food were brought in.

When these dishes were placed upon the table an army of rats came out.

There were white rats, and black rats, and brown rats, and big rats, and little rats.

At once they fell upon the food and ate it nearly all up.

"Why do you let the rats do this?" asked the captain.

"Alas, we cannot help ourselves," said the king. "I would give half my kingdom to be rid of them."

Then the captain thought of Dick Whittington's cat.

"I have an animal which will rid you of them," said the captain.

"Pray bring it in at once," said the queen.

What fun Dick's cat had killing the rats and mice in the king's palace!

"We must buy that little animal," said the queen. "I do not care how much she may cost."

The captain could hardly carry all the jewels and gold that the king gave him for the cat.

Then the ship with Dick's money came back to London, and the captain told the story to Mr. Fitzwarren.

"We must take these jewels and all this gold at once to Mr. Whittington," said the honest man. "He is no longer a poor boy, for this has made him rich."

They found Dick in the kitchen blacking the stove.

"Come with me at once into the parlor," said Mr. Fitzwarren.

Then the bags of gold and jewels were piled at Dick's feet.

"See what your cat has brought you," said Mr. Fitzwarren. "You are now a rich man and may yet be Lord Mayor of London."

And it is true that after Dick Whittington became a man, he was made Lord Mayor of London.

THE NEW MOON

Dear mother, how prettyThe moon looks to-night!She was never so cunning before;Her two little hornsAre so sharp and so bright,I hope she'll not grow any more.

If I were up there,With you and my friends,I'd rock in it nicely, you'd see;I'd sit in the middleAnd hold by both ends.Oh, what a bright cradle 'twould be!

I would call to the starsTo keep out of the way,Lest we should rock over their toes;And then I would rockTill the dawn of the day,And see where the pretty moon goes.And there we would stayIn the beautiful skies,And through the bright clouds we would roam;We would see the sun set,And see the sun rise,And on the next rainbow come home.

ELIZA LEE FOLLEN

BRIAR ROSE—I

A long time ago there lived a king and queen who were very, very sad because they had no children.

One day, when the queen was resting near a spring, a frog crept out of the water and said to her:

"You shall have your wish. Within a year you shall have a little girl."

What the frog said came true.

The queen had a little child who was so beautiful that the king gave a party in her honor.

He wished to invite all the wise women in the land, for these wise women could grant fairy gifts to his little child.

There were thirteen of them, but only twelve were invited, as the king had only twelve golden plates.

After the dinner was over, the wise women in turn arose from the table and named their fairy gifts to the little princess.

The first gave to her goodness; the second, beauty; the third, riches; and so on, up to the last.

Before the twelfth wise woman could speak, in walked the thirteenth.

This woman was in a great rage because she had not been invited.

She cried in a loud voice, "When the princess is fifteen years old she shall prick her finger with a spindle and shall fall down dead."

At these words every one turned pale with fright.

The twelfth wise woman, who had not yet spoken, now came up and said:

"I could not stop this woman's evil words, I can only make them less harsh.

The king's child shall not die, but a deep sleep shall fall upon her, in which she shall stay one hundred years."

BRIAR ROSE—II

The little princess was so beautiful, so kind; and so good that no one who knew her could help loving her.

As she grew older the king and queen began to feel very unhappy, for they could not help thinking of what was to happen to their dear little daughter.

They ordered all the spindles in the kingdom to be burned.

Now, as it happened, on the very day that the princess was fifteen years old the king and queen were away from home.

The princess was quite alone in the castle, and she rain about over the palace, looking in at rooms and halls, just as her fancy led her.

At last she came to an old tower at the top of a winding stair.

She saw a little door.

In the lock was a rusty key.

When she turned it, the door flew open.

There, in a small room, sat an old woman with her spindle, spinning flax.

24

"Good Morning," said the princess. "Do tell me what that funny thing is that jumps about so."

And then she held out her hand to take the spindle.

It came about just as the fairy had foretold.

The princess pricked her finger with the spindle.

At once she fell upon a bed which was near, and lay in a deep sleep as if dead.

This sleep came not only upon the princess, but spread over the whole castle.

The king and queen, who had just come home, fell asleep, and all their lords and ladies with them.

The horses went to sleep in the stable; the dogs in the yard; the doves on the roof; the flies on the wall; yes, even the fire that burned in the fireplace grew still and slept.

The meat stopped roasting before the fire.

The cook in the kitchen was just going to box the ears of the kitchen boy, but her hand dropped and she sank to sleep.

Outside the castle the wind was still, and upon the trees not a leaf stirred.

In a short time there sprung up around the castle a hedge of thorn bushes.

Year by year the hedge grew higher and higher, until at last nothing of the castle could be seen above it, not even the roof, nor the chimneys, nor the flag on the tower.

BRIAR ROSE—III

As years went by the story of the sleeping beauty was told all over the kingdom.

Many kings' sons came and tried to get through the hedge of thorns, but this they could not do.

The sharp thorns seemed to have hands which held the young men fast.

After many, many years a prince came from a far-off kingdom.

He heard the story of the castle and its sleeping beauty.

He knew what danger lay in the great hedge of thorn bushes.

But the young prince was brave, and he was not to be turned back.

"I am not afraid. I will go out and see this beautiful Briar Rose," he said.

It happened that the hundred years of the magic spell had just ended.

The day had come when the sleeping princess was to wake up again.

As the prince came to the hedge of thorn bushes, it was in full bloom and covered with beautiful red flowers. There, through the thorn bushes, lay a wide road.

Soon the prince came to the gates of the castle.

He found the horses and dogs lying asleep on the ground.

The doves sat on the roof with their heads under their wings.

He went into the castle.

Even the flies on the wall still slept.

Near the throne lay the king and queen, while all around were the sleeping lords and ladies.

The whole castle was so still that he could hear his heart beat.

The prince went on from room to room until he came to the old tower.

Going up the winding stair he saw the little door.

A rusty key was in the lock, and the door was half open.

There before him lay the sleeping princess.

The prince bent down and gave her a kiss.

As he did so the sleeping beauty opened her eyes. With her the whole castle awoke.

The king waked up, and the queen, and all the lords and ladies.

The horses in the stable stood up and shook themselves.

The dogs jumped about and wagged their tails.

The doves on the roof lifted their heads and flew into the fields.

The flies on the wall began to buzz.

The fire in the kitchen began to burn.

The meat began to roast.

The cook boxed the ears of the kitchen boy, so that he ran off crying.

The hedge of thorn bushes around the castle dried up and blew away.

Then the prince married the beautiful princess, and they lived happily ever after.

WILLIAM AND JACOB GRIMM

ALL THINGS BEAUTIFUL

All things bright and beautiful,All creatures great and small,All things wise and wonderful,The Lord God made them all.

Each little flower that opens,Each little bird that sings,He made their glowing colors,He made their tiny wings.

The cold wind in the winter,The pleasant summer sun,The ripe fruits in the garden,He made them every one.

He gave us eyes to see them,And lips that we might tellHow great is God Almighty,Who hath made all things well.

MRS. C.F. ALEXANDER

THE BAKER BOYS AND THE BEES—I

t rouble	An dernach	g uarded

Long years ago many cities had great stone walls around them.

The walls were built to keep out enemies, for in those old days cities often went to war with one another.

The city of Andernach had around it one of these great walls.

There was only one gateway into the city, and this gateway was guarded by strong iron doors.

Just behind the doors lived a gatekeeper, who did nothing but open and shut the gates.

He watched them well.

No one could come in who was not friendly to the city.

The gates were not opened very often. Some days they were not opened at all. So the gatekeeper had much spare time.

"I am very fond of honey," thought he. "I think I will buy a few hives of bees. I can place the hives on the top of the wall. There nobody will trouble them."

Soon there were rows of beehives on the top of the wall over the gate.

It happened that, not far away, there was another walled city, named Lintz.

The people of Lintz were the enemies of the people of Andernach.

They were always watching each other, and fought when they could get a chance.

Now the people of Lintz planned to attack and capture the city of Andernach.

They called their wisest men together to see how the attack should be made.

Many plans were talked over.

At length an old man said, "Men of Lintz, you know that the men of Andernach are lazy. They like to lie late in their beds. If we attack the city at sunrise, we shall capture it before they can get their eyes open."

This plan seemed wise to the people of Lintz, and in army was soon ready to march against the city of Andernach.

One dark night the army crept softly toward the walls of the sleeping city.

THE BAKER BOYS AND THE BEES—II

The only people who rose early in Andernach were the bakers. They had to have fresh bread ready for breakfast.

After their work was done the bakers used to have a morning nap, but the baker boys had to stay awake and watch the loaves of bread.

Two of these boys, named Hans and Fritz, were fast friends and were always together.

One morning, just at sunrise, Hans said to Fritz, "Let us creep upon the wall over the gatekeeper's house. I think we can find some honey. The old gatekeeper is asleep; he will not hear us."

The two boys crept softly up the stairs.

They soon reached the top of the wall.

"Did you hear that noise?" whispered Fritz.

"Yes, it must be the old gatekeeper," said Hans, in a low voice.

"No, it seems to come from over the wall," said Fritz.

The two boys crawled to the edge of the wall and carefully looked over.

There stood the army of Lintz.

A ladder was placed against the wall.

The soldiers would soon mount over the gate into the city.

What was to be done?

There was no time to wake the people.

What could two boys do against an army?

In an instant Fritz thought of the beehives.

Ah, the bees were awake if the people were not!

Each boy seized a hive and bore it carefully to the edge of the wall.

Then with a strong push down tumbled hives, honey, and bees upon the heads of the enemy.

Such buzzing, such stinging, such shouting as arose!

The boys ran down the stairs to the city hall.

The old bell ringer was aroused by the cries.

Soon the wild clang of the bell awoke the people of Andernach.

Armed men ran to the city gate, but the bees had done their work well. There was no need for soldiers.

The army of Lintz was running away.

Over the great gate the people of Andernach placed a statue of the two baker boys whose quick wit had saved the city.

German Folk Tale

FALLING SNOW

See the pretty snowflakesFalling from the sky;On the wall and housetopsSoft and thick they lie.

On the window ledges,On the branches bare;Now how fast they gather,Filling all the air.

Look into the garden,Where the grass was green;Covered by the snowflakes,Not a blade is seen.

Now the bare black bushesAll look soft and white,Every twig is laden,—What a pretty sight!

ANONYMOUS

LITTLE GOODY TWO SHOES

All the world must know that Two Shoes was not her real name. No; her father's name was Meanwell, and he was for many years a well-to-do farmer.

While Margery (for that was her real name) was yet a little girl her father became very poor. He was so poor that at last he and Margery's mother and Margery and her little brother were all turned out of doors. They did not have a roof to cover their heads.

Margery's father felt so unhappy that at last he died, and only a few days later Margery's mother died, too. Poor little Margery and her brother were left alone in the wide world.

Their sorrow would have made you pity them, but it would have done your heart good to see how fond they were of each other. They always went about hand in hand, and when you saw one you were sure to see the other.

27

Look at them in the picture.

They were both very ragged, and though Tommy had two shoes, Margery had but one. They had nothing, poor little things, to live upon but what kind people gave to them. Each night they lay on the hay in just such a barn as you see here.

LITTLE GOODY TWO SHOES—II

Mr. Smith was a very good man who lived in the town where little Margery and Tommy were born. Although he was a poor man, he took the children home to live with him.

"They shall not want for food nor for a bed to sleep in while I live," he said.

Mr. Smith had a friend who was a very wealthy man. When he heard the story about Margery and Tommy, this man gave Mr. Smith some money to buy little Margery a new pair of shoes and Tommy a new suit of clothes. Can you see Tommy in the picture wearing his new clothes?

The gentleman who had given the money for Margery's new shoes and Tommy's new clothes wished to take Tommy with him to London to make a sailor of him.

When the time came for Tommy to go, both children began to cry. They kissed each other a hundred times. At last Tommy wiped away Margery's tears and said:

"Don't cry, little sister, for I will come home to you again and bring you beautiful clothes and much money."

That night Margery went to bed weeping for her dear little brother. It was the first time they had ever been parted.

The next morning the shoemaker came in with Margery's new shoes. She put them on in great glee and ran out to Mrs. Smith crying, "Two shoes, two shoes. See goody two shoes!" This she did to all the people she met, so that soon she was known far and wide as Goody Two Shoes.

LITTLE GOODY TWO SHOES—III

Dear little Margery saw how good and wise Mr. Smith was. She thought it was because he read so many books.

Soon Margery wished, above all things, to learn to read. She would borrow books from the school children and sit down and read and read. Very soon she could read better than any of her playmates.

Margery took such delight in her books that she wished everybody else could read, too, so she formed this plan of teaching very little children how to read.

First, she made letters out of bits of wood with her knife. She worked and worked until there were ten sets of the small letters:

a b c d e f g h i j k l m n o p q r s t u v w x y z

and six sets of the large letters:

A B C D E F G H I J K L M N O P Q R S T U V W X Y Z

She then made the little tots spell words with her wooden letters. Take the word "plum-pudding" (and who can think of a better one!); the first little child picked up the letter p, the next l, the next u, the next m, and so on, until the whole word was spelled.

If a child took up a wrong letter, he was to pay a fine or play no more.

Each morning, with her basket full of wooden letters, Margery went around from house to house. The little children learned to read very fast.

Can you see Margery with her basket of letters in this picture?

The first house she came to was Farmer Wilson's. See, here it is.

Margery stopped and ran up to the door. Tap, tap, tap.

"Who is there?"

"Only little Goody Two Shoes," said Margery, "come to teach Billy."

"Is that you, little Goody?" said Mrs. Wilson. "I am glad to see you."

Then out came the little boy.

"How do, Doody Two Shoes," said he, not being able to speak plainly.

28

Margery took little Billy by the hand and led him to a quiet spot under a tree. Then she threw the letters on the ground all mixed up together like this:

z a y w b m p j f x c o q g e k v n i d h r i t u s

Billy picked them up, calling each one by its right name, and put them all in just their right places. They now looked like this:

a b c d e f g h i j k l m n o p q r s t u v w x y z

Do you think you could have done as well as little Billy?

The next place Margery came to was Farmer Simpson's, and here it is.

"Bowwow, wow," said the dog at the door.

"Be still, sir," said Mrs. Simpson. "Why do you bark at little Two Shoes? Come, Alice, here is Goody Two Shoes ready to teach you."

Then out came the little one.

"Well, Alice," said Two Shoes, "have you learned your lesson?"

"Yes, indeed, I have," said the little one, and taking the letters, she formed them in this way:

ba be bi bo bu da de di do dufa fe fi fo fu ha he hi ho hu

As she formed them she gave their exact sounds.

The next place Margery came to was Gaffer Cook's house. Here a number of poor children all came around her at once. These children had been to her school longer than the first little tots, and could read words and lines.

This is what Margery gave them to read:

"He that will thrive must rise by five."

"Truth can be blamed, but cannot be shamed."

"A friend in your need is a friend indeed."

"A wise head makes a close mouth."

"A lie stands upon one leg, but truth upon two."

"A good boy will make a good man."

"Honor your parents and the world will honor you."

"Love your friends and your friends will love you."

Did you ever read lines like these in your school reader?

LITTLE GOODY TWO SHOES—IV

At last Margery grew up and was given a real school to teach and a real schoolroom to teach in. She still used her little wooden letters, and made the children fetch each one to spell the words.

One day, as Margery was going home from school, she saw some bad boys who had caught a young crow. She went over to them and gave them a penny for the poor little bird, and took him home.

Margery called the crow Ralph, and under her care he grew into a very fine bird indeed. She even taught him to speak and to pick out a few of the letters.

Some time after this a poor lamb had lost his mother, and the farmer was about to kill him. Margery bought him and took him home with her to play with the children. This lamb she called Will, and a pretty fellow he was. Do look at him. See him run and play with the children.

The lamb was trained to carry home the books and the slates of the children who behaved well at school. See what a fine, strong fellow he is, and how he trudges along.

Margery also had a present of a little dog. His name was Jumper. Look at him sitting up and begging in the picture.

Did you ever see a dog with such bright eyes? He almost seems able to talk.

Jumper, Jumper, Jumper! He was always playing and jumping about, and Jumper was a good name for him. His place was just outside the door. See how he sits, the saucy fellow!

LITTLE GOODY TWO SHOES—V

One day Jumper came whining into the schoolroom. He took hold of Margery's dress and pulled and pulled.

"What do you wish, dear Jumper?" asked Margery.

But the dog only whined and pulled her toward the door. At last Margery went outdoors to see what was the matter.

Then Jumper left her and ran back into the schoolroom. He took hold of the dress of one of the little girls and tugged and tugged. At length she too followed Jumper to the door.

By this time all the children were on their feet and quickly followed the teacher out of the schoolroom.

They were none too soon. The last little girl had hardly passed the door when, with a great crash, the roof fell in.

All the children were safe, but what had become of Margery's dear books and letters and other things?

Margery did not lose her school. A rich man who lived near ordered the schoolhouse to be rebuilt at his own expense.

Another gentleman, Sir Charles Jones, having heard of Margery's good sense, offered her a home if she would teach his daughter. In fact he finally fell in love with Margery, and they were married in the great church. And what do you think! On her wedding day, while the bells were ringing, Margery's brother Tommy came home. He had become the captain of a great ship. He had sailed to many lands, and he brought her all kinds of presents. Do you think she deserved to be very happy?

She did not forget the children, you may be sure. A house in the village was fitted up as a school, and all the boys and girls were taught to read and write.

Ascribed to GOLDSMITH

ONE STEP AND THEN ANOTHER

One step and then another,And the longest walk is ended;One stitch and then another,And the largest rent is mended.

One brick upon another,And the highest wall is made;One flake upon another,And the deepest snow is laid.

ANONYMOUS

GOOD NIGHT AND GOOD MORNING

c	n	c
urious	eighed	urtsied

A fair little girl sat under a tree,Sewing as long as her eyes could see;Then smoothed her work and folded it right,And said, "Dear work, good night, good night!"

Such a number of rooks came over her head,Crying "Caw, caw!" on their way to bed.She said, as she watched their curious flight,"Little black things, good night, good night!"

The horses neighed, and the oxen lowed,The sheep's "bleat, bleat!" came over the road;All seeming to say, with a quiet delight,"Good little girl, good night, good night!"

She did not say to the sun, "Good night!"Though she saw him there like a ball of light,For she knew he had God's time to keepAll over the world, and never could sleep.

The tall pink foxglove bowed his head;The violets curtsied and went to bed;And good little Lucy tied up her hair,And said, on her knees, her favorite prayer.

And while on her pillow she softly lay,She knew nothing more till again it was day;And all things said to the beautiful sun,"Good morning, good morning! our work is begun."

LORD HOUGHTON

DAVID AND GOLIATH—I

Ph	g	G
ilistines	uarding	oliath

Long, long ago there lived, in the country of Israel a boy named David.

He was a shepherd boy, and all day long he watched the quiet sheep as they ate sweet grass on the hillside.

Although David was only a boy, he was tall and strong and brave.

When he knew he was in the right, he feared nothing.

David's quiet life did not last long.

There was a great war between the people of Israel and men called the Philistines.

All the strong men in David's town went to join the army of Israel.

David could not go, as he had to tend the sheep, but his three older brothers went to the war.

For a long time David's father heard nothing from his three oldest boys.

At length he called David to him and said, "Take to your brothers a bag of this corn and these ten loaves of bread. Find out how your brothers are, and bring word to me."

The next morning David rose very early, and taking the bag of corn and the loaves of bread, he went to the camp where his brothers were.

The camp of Israel was on the side of a high mountain.

Across the valley from this mountain and on the side of another mountain was the camp of the Philistines.

After David had come to the camp and had found his brothers, shouts of anger and fear came from the soldiers.

David looked across the valley to the camp of the Philistines.

There he saw a huge soldier dressed in shining armor.

This giant soldier carried a great spear and shield.

"Who is that man?" asked David.

"Do you not know? That is Goliath," said the soldiers. "Every day he comes out and dares any man on our side to meet him in battle."

"Does no one of our soldiers dare to meet him?" asked David.

"We have no man so strong as he in our whole army," said the soldiers.

The giant from the opposite hillside shouted with a loud voice, and again dared the army of Israel to choose a man to meet him.

David was a brave boy; he was stirred to anger at the sight of this great giant.

"Is not God on the side of our people?" he asked. "I will fight with this man, even though he kill me."

DAVID AND GOLIATH—II

The king of Israel heard of these brave words and sent for David to come before him.

When he saw that David was only a boy, he said, "You are not able to go against this Philistine. You are only a boy, while he has fought in many battles."

Then David said to the king, "Once, when I was guarding my father's sheep, I killed a lion and a bear without help from any one but the Lord. He will help me fight this man."

Then the king said, "Go, and the Lord be with you."

The king fitted David with heavy armor and gave to him his own sword, but David said, "I am not used to this heavy armor; it will only hinder me."

So he threw it off.

Then David went to a brook near by and chose five smooth stones.

Armed with these five stones and his sling; he went bravely out to meet the giant.

When the giant saw that David was only a boy, he was angry and cried out:

"Do you dare fight with me? I will kill you, and will give your flesh to the birds and the beasts."

31

David looked at him without fear and said, "You come against me with a sword and with a spear and with a shield, but I come to you in the name of the Lord. This day will he give you into my hand. I will kill you and take your head from you, and I will give the bodies of the Philistines to the birds and the beasts."

When they came near to each other, David fitted one of the five stones to his sling.

He whirled the sling swiftly about his head. The stone flew straight to its mark. It struck the Philistine full in the forehead. The huge giant took one step and, with a groan, fell to the earth.

Then David, standing upon the giant, took his sword and cut off the head of his enemy.

When the Philistines saw that their giant was dead, they were filled with fear.

They left their camp and tried to run away, but the army of Israel followed them and won a great victory.

For this brave deed David was made a captain and was held in honor by the king.

Adapted from the Bible

PHONETIC TABLES

The following tables are planned to supplement those already developed in the "Beacon Primer" and in the "Beacon First Reader."

The earlier tables are introduced in order that the teacher may have them for rapid review work with her slower pupils, and also for those pupils entering the class without any previous phonetic training.

The strictly new matter, which includes the last ten pages, should receive special emphasis and care in its development and drill.

REVIEW OF THE VOWELS *a, e, i, o,* and *u*

ix	ut	ob	ig	ag
id	ug	in	an	et
og	ab	og	od	ex
ed	ox	ix	ax	ud

es	ug	id	it	ix
ug	im	ell	ed	ox
eg	ug	in	ed	ill
uff	ug	ess	ub	im

In the following words a blend of two consonants follows the vowel.

elt	ilt	lm	lk	elf

32

ilt	ick	ich	oft	ink
ilk	ank	est	ilt	ish
ock	imp	uft	ilt	ick
ust	ulk	elt	int	ust
and	ush	ilt	elt	ack
ick	ack	ent	ent	ist
ink	unt	ash	end	ush
ash	ush	ust	uck	uch
ing	usk	ing	ond	ulk
ent	unk	ack	ick	ank
esk	ank	int	elt	ing
ack	ink	ulk	ent	ent
amp	ust	ock	ack	and
ind	ump	ick	uck	unk
unt	ock	usk	and	uch
ump	ush	end	ump	end
ump	ump	ond	usk	amp

In the following words a blend of two consonants precedes the vowel. The vowel must be sounded with the preceding consonants.

led	log	lag	lip	liff
rit	lip	rin	rog	rip
lat	rot	rill	tiff	lop
pot	lot	rig	led	till
niff	rip	lap	lab	can
cud	wit	tep	pin	rag
pan	rab	tag	len	rag
lum	tab	rag	rim	kill
kim	lim	lad	rop	rop
nuff	kin	kip	cab	nob
kull	nip	led	tun	win
ress	rab	rill	kiff	rom
well	rug	wig	rim	nap
cum	ran	tub	nag	tem
lum	ped	pill	rop	lam
rum	ruff	nug	ress	nub
mell	pell	rim	less	pun

The correct pronunciation of *wh* is important. In reality the *h* is sounded before the *w*, and in the oldest English it was so written. This table combines the features of the two previous tables.

ᵛ it	ᶜ hip	lock	ᶜ rank	heft
ᵛ hit	ˢ hut	rick	ˢ hock	ling
ᵛ het	ˢ hed	helf	ᵗ runk	rust
ᵛ hig	ˢ hop	wift	ᵖ lank	ting
ᵛ hip	ˢ had	rock	ˢ wing	resh
ᵛ hiff	ᶜ hub	trap	ˢ mith	wist
ᵛ hen	ˢ hun	rick	ˢ tring	rack
ᵛ hist	ᵗ rash	rick	ˢ mack	rash
ᵛ him	ᶜ hest	rust	ˢ tump	tock
ᵛ hich	ˢ cript	crub	ˢ plash	crap
ᵛ hisk	ˢ pend	hred	ˢ truck	lock
ˢ hip	ᶜ ramp	runt	ˢ camp	rank
ᶜ hill	ˢ mash	rint	ˢ hrink	hrob
ᶜ hat	ᵗ witch	tack	ᵗ hump	luck
ˢ prang	ˢ pring	rink	ᵗ hrush	hrub
ˢ ham	ˢ witch	heck	ˢ tretch	rush
ᶜ hess	ˢ natch	hank	ˢ cratch	pank

In the following words the vowel is long because of the final *e*.

ᵗ			ᶠ	ᶜ

ide	ote	ite	ade	ore
ᵍore	ute	ive	ᵗrade	ᵍlide
ᵗone	ole	ive	ˡlate	ᵛore
ᶜope	obe	ore	ᶜrave	ᶜrive
ᵗube	ane	ive	ˢpore	ᶠride
˅ipe	ide	ave	ᵍlobe	ˢtove
ˢlate	ore	ave	ˢnipe	ˢnore
ʳere	lake	ove	ˢtone	ˢpine
ˢtore	tole	ave	ᶠlame	ᵗlade
ʳute	ide	tale	ᵍrove	ᶜrime
ˢtake	one	ete	ᵍrape	ˢhave
ˢkate	ine	ake	ˢmite	ᵍrime
ˢpike	ore	ave	˅hite	ˢtride
ᵇrake	core	lope	ᶜrone	ˢpade
ˢpoke	ume	trife	ᵗwine	ˢhape
ˢnake	ade	lime	ˢtrive	ᵛhale
ˢtrike	lave	ode	ˢtripe	ᵗlame
ˢtroke	hine	mile	ˢwore	ˢcrape

36

moke	hade	hore	hame	hrone

The following words illustrate the effect of final *e* in lengthening the vowel otherwise short. Final *se* usually has the sound of *ze*.

ot	ote	lat	late	laze
ob	obe	rip	ripe	ose
ut	ute	lid	lide	oze
ot	ote	rip	ripe	use
ot	ote	lop	lope	aze
ub	ube	hin	hine	ose
on	one	lim	lime	roze
ub	ube	lad	lade	hese
od	ode	nip	nipe	aze
et	ete	hot	hote	ise
lat	late	pin	pine	ize
lam	lame	lan	lane	ise
had	hade	trip	tripe	aze
op	ope	rim	rime	ose
hit	hite	win	wine	aze
ham	hame	rim	rime	hose

crap	crape	lum	lume	lose

Before *r* the sounds of the vowels *a, e, i,* and *u* are greatly modified. These combinations occur so frequently that much drill is required. Final *e* affects *ar* as in *care.*

tir	erf	ar	ar	ur
lur	art	art	ur	url
tar	urf	irst	url	ird
erk	ard	ern	ird	art
irm	car	ard	har	par
url	ark	urt	art	rch
urn	lur	urr	ert	pur
ard	arn	arn	arp	erd
ark	urn	erm	ark	ard
tart	hirt	ark	arn	arp
harp	lerk	kirt	hirp	ark
park	hark	ark	purt	hird
arch	mart	hurn	erch	arm
harm	tarch	arch	irth	mirch

are	care	are	are	are
are	nare	are	are	lare

38

are	pare	are	tare	hare

In the words of this table *ea* and *ee* have the long sound of *e*.

f ear	t ear	l ean	h eap	f leet
t hee	e ast	e ase	k eep	b eef
r ear	p lea	h eed	g reet	y ear
f reed	d ean	t eam	w eed	r eam
t ease	d eed	t reat	w ean	t each
s heet	y east	m eet	s pree	p lead
s heaf	m ead	s teep	s heer	e aves
g reed	c reak	c reek	s hear	s pear
b reed	a gree	s neer	b leed	s peed
b each	s heen	g reen	p reen	c heap
s weep	s heep	r each	s treet	f reeze
c ream	t weed	f leece	c ream	w eave
s creen	p each	g leam	w heat	s treak
b ream	l eaves	c leans	c rease	t eapot
b eams	p lease	g reedy	E aster	s pleen
b reeze	g leans	s queak	b eaver	s eason
g	s	w	s	s

rease	neeze	heeze	heath	tream
r eason	t eacher	s heaves	s cream	b eacon

In the words of this table *ai* and *ay* have the long sound of *a*.

ail	ain	ail	ail	lail
lay	ray	ail	ait	rail
ain	ail	ray	lay	aid
ray	ray	ain	ail	ray
aise	aint	tray	nail	aint
taid	way	aint	aith	rain
ayly	pray	hain	lain	aid
tain	train	aist	raid	rain
rain	raise	trait	wain	laim
way	prain	aisin	fraid	ainty

In the words of this table *oa* and *oe* have the long sound of *o*.

ats	oar	loe	oar	oat
oax	loat	ak	oal	oap
oam	oed	oad	oan	oak
hoa	oam	oat	oat	oat
loak	oarse	oam	oast	oast

40

roan	hroat	hoal	roak	oast
oaves	oarse	oan	oach	oard

In the words of this table *ie* and final *y* take the long sound of *i*.

ie	ie	ly	ry	hy
ie	ty	ry	hy	ied
ried	ky	ied	ied	ried
ried	lly	ely	efy	eny
eply	pry	kies	lies	ried
upply	pied	lied	ried	omply

In the words of this table *ew* and *ue* are pronounced very nearly like *u* long.

ue	ue	tew	ew	ue
ew	ew	iew	gue	ewel
escue	inew	rgue	ubdue	alue
ildew	ewter	enew	teward	nsue

In the words of this table *oi* and *oy* are pronounced alike.

oy	oil	oin	oin	oil
oil	oist	oil	oin	loy
oint	roil	oist	oist	oint
njoy	oice	oyal	oise	poil
oist	void	hoice	nnoy	oily

41

e	‘	a	p	p
mploy	yster	noint	oison	oiler

In the words of this table *au* and *aw* take the sound of *a* in *all*.

	c	ł	l	f
aw	law	aul	aul	law
aun	awn (y)	awl (ł)	haw (t)	law (s)
ault	awk (h)	aub (‘)	aud (ł)	raud (f)
awn	auze (g)	ault (‘)	rawl (ł)	ause (c)
awn	rawl (d)	awn (ſ)	awful (ł)	rawl (c)
wful	auper (p)	traw (s)	rawn (ł)	rawn (c)
ause	wning (a)	awyer (l)	pawn (s)	aucus (c)

In the words of this table *ou* and *ow* are pronounced alike.

		s	p	s
out (ℓ)	out (ı)	cow	out	cour
own (t)	rout (ı)	cout (s)	own (d)	hout (s)
row (ſ)	loud (‘)	nout (s)	ower (t)	roud (p)
lour (ſ)	outh (ı)	cowl (s)	ouch (p)	ount (rr)
tout (s)	pout (ı)	loud (a)	ower (p)	ound (b)
ount (‘)	bout (ı)	rowd (c)	ound (p)	rouch (c)
owel (t)	ouch (‘)	ound (s)	louse (b)	evout (d)
ound (ſ)	rowl (ı)	rown (f)	rouse (g)	ound (w)
lown (‘)	owel (‘)	rown (d)	prout (s)	hroud (s)

In the following list of words *oo* is pronounced like *u* in *rude*.

b oot	c ool	t ool	p ool	r oof
F oor	¹ oot	t oot	l oop	l oon
s oon	¹ ood	ᵏ oot	b oor	r ood
n oon	c oop	ᵏ oop	h oof	c oon
l oom	¹ oose	r oor	b oon	s loop
F roof	⁵ toop	t roop	s tool	s pool
b oost	¹ oose	s ooth	r oom	b oom
c roon	¹ oon	r ood	r oost	s hoot
b room	c oom	g oose	s coop	t ooth
b loom	l rood	g loom	g room	s woop
s woon	⁵ poon	r oose	c hoose	g roove

Review the sound of *qu*.

q uilt	c uid	q uill	e quip	q uit
q uell	c uite	q uiz	q uire	q uail
q ueer	c uote	q uest	q uick	s quire
s quirt	c ueen	q uince	q uake	s quint
s quaw	c uack	s quirm	s quare	q uaint

s queak	s queal	q uench	s queeze	s quirrel

REVIEW

s ly	c ard	l oft	d ue	e ar
s tir	w hy	c liff	t ied	c ue
j aw	t urn	c url	h ilt	c oil
b oil	t ube	c loy	c lay	n ail
l ute	m ail	r ose	s par	c rag
s lay	p aul	fl aw	h oof	h aul
f irm	q uill	g ore	p ray	s ank
b oot	w ore	s tew	h erd	h eap
s tun	s tem	f ried	t win	t ried
s cow	b less	s mile	n ew	t erm
t rout	m ere	g lean	f roze	g lide
s tore	s lave	s heaf	t eam	m ore
q uite	n oise	m ode	d aub	b oom
s hore	s toop	m end	s core	g auze
s heet	m uch	c hain	s tone	g rime
g runt	h awk	m oon	p awn	s hark
p	p	q	b	q

44

ump	each	uick	lock	uack
s nake	s ound	p ouch	q ueen	m arch
s mash	c ramp	s tump	s moke	s witch
s ky	g lare	r ely	r oom	t ress
s kill	d oily	g ruff	p lied	r oyal
g ayly	t ooth	sl oop	s crap	s care
s nare	e nsue	c oast	s purt	p ried
c roak	p erch	s trife	t wain	s trait
g rowl	f lower	n oose	s tripe	g auze
a wful	p ower	p arch	a nnoy	s mart
s trive	m oose	s tride	c hoice	b lame
c hurn	l oaves	a fraid	s tarch	t hroat
s inew	b eaver	r escue	c oarse	o yster
p raise	p oison	t eapot	l awful	s prain
s truck	b reezy	h oarse	a noint	s queal
s creen	s prout	g roove	c hoose	s quint
s crape	s hower	g rouse	t witch	b louse
s upply	s tretch	c aucus	d ainty	t hrone

p auper	s hroud	s eason	r eason	s quare
a uburn	t eacher	s ubdue	s prawl	f reezer
a wning	m ildew	e mploy	s mirch	. p ewter
s queeze	s quirrel	p reacher	s quirm	c omply

In the following list of words *c* is soft before *e* or *i*.

ite	a ce	i ce	c ell	c ent
ice	r ice	l ace	c ity	s ince
ice	t rice	c ice	f arce	f ence
lice	ſ ace	r ice	v oice	l ance
rice	t race	g race	ſ ence	m ince
ruce	r ace	c ease	h ence	p rince
lace	b race	f leece	c ance	t hence
pace	t wice	ſ eace	g lance	c hance
plice	s pruce	c hoice	c uince	w hence

In the following list of words *g* and *dg* before *e* and *i* are pronounced like *j*.

g in	g ist	g ill	g em	g ibe
g erm	t inge	e dge	u rge	h uge
s erge	j udge	s inge	l edge	l arge
b arge	f udge	l odge	d odge	r idge

c ringe	l unge	t udge	h edge	b adge
s ledge	r udge	w edge	f ringe	r ange
b ridge	r erge	g rudge	t rudge	n ange
s mudge	c harge	p lunge	d redge	c hange

K and *ck* are sounded exactly alike. Their use is not so confusing from the point of view of sounding as from spelling. The use of the *ck* after a short vowel should be strongly emphasized by the teacher.

ick	ike	lake	leck	lick
ake	ock	eck	eek	lock
ack	oke	lick	hock	oke
rack	ack	ock	nake	eck
tuck	lack	leek	trike	rack
reak	luck	ruck	troke	rake
rake	hake	lack	truck	neak
poke	weak	roke	mack	huck

ake	ake	ike	eak	toke
ack	ack	ick	eck	tock
ake	lake	ike	uke	moke
ack	lack	ick	uck	mock

ake	take	eak	uke	roak ᶜ
ack	tack	eck	uck	rock ᶜ
ake	ike	peak	oke	loak ᶜ
ack	ick	peck	ock	lock ᶜ

Tch generally has the same sound as *ch*. *Ch* usually follows vowels having the long sound, while *tch* usually follows vowels having the short sound.

ᵉach	ᵗeach	ˡeach	ʳeach	ˢpeech
ᵇleach	ˢcreech	ˡeech	ᵇreach	ᵇeech
ᶜoach	ʳoach	ˡoach	ᵇroach	ᵖreach
ᶠetch	ˢtretch	ⁱtch	ᵇotch	ⁿotch
ᵇlotch	ᶜatch	ˢketch	ᶜrutch	ᵖitch
ˡatch	ᵇatch	ˢnatch	ᵈitch	ⁿatch
ᵇatch	ᵖatch	ˡutch	ᵗwitch	ᶜlutch
ˢwitch	ʷitch	ˢtitch	ˢcratch	ᶠlitch

This table contains a further development of the two sounds of *th*.

ᶠifth	ᵗenth	ˢtrength	ᵗhud	ᵗhill
ᵗhing	ᵗhump	ᵗhick	ᵗhank	ᵗhatch
ᵗhrob	ᵗhrone	ᵗhrust	ᵗhrash	ᵗhrush
ᵗhis	ᵗhus	ᵗhese	ᵗhose	ᵗhat
ᵗhem	ᵗhan	ᵗhen	ᵗhe	ᵗhee

^{t}hy	^{t}athe	^{l}athe	^{s}eethe	^{l}ithe
^{b}lithe	^{v}ithe	^{c}lothe	^{s}cathe	^{t}hine
^{b}reathe	^{s}oothe	^{s}mooth	^{t}hence	^{s}heathe

In the following list of words *ie* has the sound of long *e*.

ield	iece	riest	iece	^{s}hield
rief	ield	iege	hief	^{r}elief
rief	hief	iend	hriek	^{b}elieve

In the following list of words *o* has a sound midway between its sound in *for* and in *fox*.

ost	oss	ong	roth	^{f}rost
oft	oss	ong	loth	^{s}trong
ost	oss	ong	roth	^{l}oft

In the following list of words *a* has the sound of short *o*.

as	and	wap	hat	^{s}wamp
ad	ash	wan	ant	^{w}ander
an	asp	wab	atch	^{w}asher

Two vowels together are often sounded separately.

uel	oem	iant	uiet	uel
oet	dea	ruel	ruant	uet
iet	eal	rial	liant	ial

Tion and *sion* are pronounced *shun*.

^{r}ation	^{m}ention	^{v}ision	^{t}ension	^{s}ession

r	p	n	m	s
ation	ension	otion	ission	tation
c	f	m	p	a
ption	raction	otion	assion	ction

REVIEW

f	s	c	d	b
uel	nail	ede	efy	are
f	s	s	t	g
ield	tare	kirt	hief	ruel
t	m	r	a	l
rial	ete	oost	way	edge
m	d	g	q	f
ere	eny	race	uiet	ence
p	q	c	s	s
aint	uail	ried	hare	nore
w	n	s	j	b
hist	iece	pare	udge	raid
y	p	v	g	c
east	oem	alue	rowl	rawl
s	g	g	M	a
cowl	oose	iant	aud	rgue
g	m	y	s	d
roan	oist	awn	wore	rawl
m	c	r	s	o
irth	oach	aisin	quirt	yster
a	b	s	c	s
nnoy	oiler	train	hoice	woon
b	g	P	g	s
room	audy	riest	leans	quaw
s	w	q	r	t
neeze	hisk	uake	escue	ruant
p	p	r	c	s
oison	rince	enew	rouch	prout
d	c	f	m	g
redge	rease	lower	otion	reedy
c	c	b	m	b

hance	harm	ridge	ound	elieve
⟨s⟩ upply	⟨n⟩ ation	⟨n⟩ otion	⟨s⟩ queak	⟨s⟩ hower
⟨l⟩ awyer	⟨p⟩ lunge	⟨s⟩ quare	⟨e⟩ mploy	⟨c⟩ omply
⟨q⟩ uench	⟨a⟩ wning	⟨s⟩ tream	⟨m⟩ ildew	⟨s⟩ heaves

The following list contains words with the most common suffixes.

⟨j⟩ acket	⟨m⟩ arket	⟨v⟩ elvet	⟨tr⟩ umpet
⟨l⟩ ocket	⟨b⟩ asket	⟨ti⟩ cket	⟨th⟩ icket
⟨s⟩ ecret	⟨bl⟩ anket	⟨b⟩ racket	⟨b⟩ ucket
⟨g⟩ oblet	⟨m⟩ usket	⟨r⟩ ocket	⟨gi⟩ mlet
⟨c⟩ loset	⟨c⟩ arpet	⟨ra⟩ cket	⟨h⟩ ornet
⟨m⟩ antle	⟨c⟩ amel	⟨m⟩ odel	⟨pa⟩ rcel
⟨r⟩ avel	⟨p⟩ anel	⟨s⟩ addle	⟨tr⟩ avel
⟨s⟩ lumber	⟨c⟩ hapel	⟨c⟩ anter	⟨pi⟩ ckle
⟨l⟩ umber	⟨ci⟩ nder	⟨p⟩ rinter	⟨m⟩ aster
⟨w⟩ hisper	⟨h⟩ elper	⟨si⟩ ster	⟨co⟩ rner
⟨b⟩ arber	⟨u⟩ nder	⟨lo⟩ bster	⟨fa⟩ rmer
⟨s⟩ camper	⟨w⟩ inter	⟨n⟩ umber	⟨tu⟩ mbler
⟨b⟩ lunder	⟨je⟩ ster	⟨pi⟩ tcher	⟨m⟩ ilker
⟨f⟩ arther	⟨m⟩ onster	⟨m⟩ arble	⟨cy⟩ cle

^uncle	^thimble	^{ju}mble	^{gr}umble
^stumble	^{ti}ngle	^{ti}ckle	^{sp}eckle
^candle	ⁿⁱmble	^tumble	^{an}kle
^twinkle	^{si}ngle	^dangle	^{di}mple
^cackle	^buckle	^magic	^{pi}cnic
^handle	^bundle	^{fr}olic	^mimic
^simple	^wrinkle	^merit	^{ar}ctic
^solid	^{li}mit	^habit	ⁱⁿfant
^stupid	^{vi}sit	^spirit	^{di}stant
^rapid	^profit	^pulpit	^merchant
^timid	^ashes	^{cl}asses	^{se}rvant
^kisses	^{di}shes	^dresses	^{br}ushes
^losses	stitches	^bunches	^{wi}shes
^glasses	^matches	^{lu}nches	^{pi}nches
^fishes	^branches	^churches	^goblin
^sweeten	^cabin	^driven	^{ro}bin
^quicken	^satin	^harden	^pumpkin
^seven	ⁿapkin	^beacon	^{sh}orten

ᵇeckon	ʳᵉckon	ᵈragon	ᵇˡacken
ˢermon	ʷagon	ˡᵉmon	ᵖʳison
ˢeason	ᵐelon	ˡᵉsson	ᵐason
ᶠifty	ªngry	ᵘgly	ᵐilky
ˢixty	ˢadly	ᵈainty	ʳᵘsty
ʰungry	ᵖantry	ᵉmpty	ˢⁱˡky
ᶠinely	ˢafely	ˡªtely	ᵖªges
ᵐerely	ʷidely	ᵖurely	ᵖʳices
ⁿicely	ˡᵒnely	ᶜˡosely	ʷages
ʳaces	ˢpices	ªges	ᵖˡaces
ᶠaces	ᶜases	ᶜages	ˢᵗages
ˡaces	ᵇˡazes	ᶜˡoses	ʳᵒses
ªxes	ᵍazes	ⁿoses	ʳⁱˢes
ʰateful	ˢⁱzes	ᵘses	ᵖʳizes
ʷasteful	ʰelpful	ʳⁱval	ⁿªval
ⁿeedful	ˢpiteful	ᶠⁱnal	ᵛⁱtal
ᶜheerful	ᵗhankful	ᵒval	ᵒpal
ᵍraceful	ᵗʳuthful	ˡᵒcal	ˡᵉgal

w akeful	c areful	fl oral	fa tal

The following list contains words with the most common prefixes.

aw ake	ab ed	af loat	a dorn
afr aid	alo ud	as leep	al ert
afi re	ag o	a mid	a drift
aw ay	ab out	ag ree	al as
alo ne	acr oss	ab laze	a ward
be came	ag ain	b ecome	a part
be cause	ar ound	b egin	al ive
bel ong	alo ng	u ntwist	a buse
un hitch	aw hile	u njust	b etween
un hurt	be gan	de pend	b efall
del ay	be have	de clare	b eside
de mand	be fore	de vote	u nbend
dis play	un lock	ex cite	u ntrue
dis place	un fit	ex plode	u nchain
dis gust	un clean	ex pand	e xceed
en camp	de cay	di scharge	e xpect
en	de	di	e

rage	part	spute	xcel
enj oy	de fend	di smiss	e xpose
inq uire	en dure	di sturb	e xcuse
inc lose	enl arge	fo rbid	e xpress
inf orm	en grave	fo rgive	e xplain
int ent	ex cept	fo rget	re quire
ins ist	ex change	fo rsake	u nwind
inv ite	ex plore	re bound	b ehind
inf lame	ex claim	re cess	u nfold
re mark	re peat	re cite	re ply
ref er	re pair	re place	re call
re new	re gret	re lease	re tain
rej oice	ret urn	re duce	re port
reg ard	ref resh	re store	re main
co achman	hu ntsman	se aman	p ostman
sal esman	w orkman	fo otman	h ackman
rail road	bir thday	fo reman	b oatman
ink stand	da ylight	fir eplace	te acup

sea side	se aweed	su nbeam	ti ptoe
sta irway	ne cktie	ra inbow	ra ilway
sea shore	co bweb	sp yglass	b eehive

Usually the vowel followed by one consonant is given the long sound, whereas, when the consonant is doubled, the vowel usually has the short sound, as illustrated in the following words.

b iter	p later	t oper	h oping
b itter	p latter	s topper	h opping
d iner	s hiny	t iny	d oted
d inner	s hinny	t inny	d otted
c uter	h ater	p oker	o ffer
c utter	h ated	p aper	w ider
h oly	h atter	t aper	s pider
h olly	r iding	f avor	di ver
b ony	r idding	f ever	g allon
b onny	b iting	c lover	ra cer
b ogy	b itting	o ver	ci der
b oggy	c aning	h alo	la bel
M ary	c anning	s olo	y ellow
m arry	p laner	p olo	jo lly

m ate	p lanner	f labby	je lly
m atter	r uder	s habby	m aker
r obed	r udder	r uddy	ta ker
r obbed	l oping	t ulip	d ummy
p ining	l opping	c edar	c ommon
p inning	b aker	t amer	m oment
t uning	s hady	l iner	si lent
st unning	l ady	p acer	r uby
p laning	t idy	g iddy	b onnet
p lanning	p ony	s udden	p enny

The following words illustrate silent *k, g, w, h, l, t,* and *gh.*

k nee	k neel	k nelt	k nell	k nit
k nife	k not	k nock	k nob	k new
k nave	k nead	k now	k nack	g nat
g naw	g nu	g nash	g narl	g nome
w ry	w ren	w rist	w rote	w rite
w rap	w ring	w rung	w rong	w rest
w reck	w rath	w retch	w reak	w rench
w	w	h	si	w

rithe	reath	igh	gh	right
t high	l ight	fi ght	ti ght	s ight
k night	r ight	f right	p light	n ight
b light	s light	b right	fl ight	m ight
c aught	n aught	t aught	d aughter	a ught
ti ghtly	b rightly	li ghtly	li ghtning	n aughty
cl imb	c omb	c rumb	d umb	l amb
li mb	n umb	t humb	d ebt	d oubt
c ombing	c alf	h alf	b alm	c alm
c halk	s talk	w alk	f olks	t alk
o ften	s often	c astle	j ostle	r ustle
t histle	w histle	c hestnut	f asten	l isten

CPSIA information can be obtained
at www.ICGtesting.com
Printed in the USA
LVHW051047130723
752393LV00017B/362

9 781511 868204